# Addie Across the Prairie

## Laurie Lawlor

### Illustrated by Gail Owens

Aladdin Paperbacks
New York   London   Toronto   Sydney   Singapore

*To the real Ruby Lillian and*
*her great-grandchildren,*
*John and Megan.*

---

First Aladdin Paperbacks edition March 2002

Text copyright © 1986 by Laurie Lawlor

Illustrations copyright © 1986 by Gail Owens

Cover art copyright © 1991 by Steve Brennan

Originally published by Minstrel Books in April 1991

Published by arrangement with Albert Whitman & Company

ALADDIN PAPERBACKS
An imprint of Simon & Schuster
Children's Publishing Division
1230 Avenue of the Americas
New York, NY 10020

For information address: Albert Whitman & Company,
5747 West Howard Street, Niles, IL 60648.

Printed in the U.S.A.
16 18 20 19 17

ISBN: 0-671-70147-9

# CONTENTS

# 1 HOW LONG TILL DAKOTA?

There seemed to be no edge to the land. The very weight of the sky made Addie duck her head a little. She felt so frightened and small! She turned around and around, but every way she looked the view was the same—rolling prairie stretching for miles and miles. No trees, no houses, no real hills like the steep Mississippi bluffs back home. And at night no neighbors' friendly lights, only vast blackness.

When Addie became tired of staring at the emptiness, of trying to find something—anything—on the horizon, she dropped to her knees and let the tall grass with its sweet, dry smell swallow her up. The grasshoppers sang long, bandy-legged songs and leapt away when she moved closer for a better look. She watched battalions of dragonflies soar past, their wings glistening in the bright October morning sunlight. Absent-mindedly, Addie dug her fingers down into the sod, the dense mat of dead grass and roots and black earth. Aphids, ants, and grubs burrowed frantically out of reach. Were they trying to hide from the enormous sky the way she was?

The dry Indian grass and switch grass rustled, seeming to whisper, "Who are you? What are you doing here?"

Addie did not answer. Lying back in the grass, she looked straight up into the sky and watched the clouds chase each other. She thought about her best friend, Eleanor. Back in Jackson County, Iowa, was Eleanor thinking about her?

Addie shut her eyes and imagined her friend balancing on the fence between their two farms back home. "Addie, Addie, fraidycat!" Eleanor called down, laughing, her blonde hair flying wild in the wind. "Come on up and say hello!" Addie knew walking the old rail fence was dangerous. But Eleanor's words made her flush with anger and embarrassment. She didn't like it when Eleanor reminded her she wasn't brave or bold or daring.

She and Eleanor were both nine years old and had been friends and neighbors for as long as Addie could remember. They did everything and went everywhere together, even though they were as different as two friends could be. Eleanor was fair-haired, blue-eyed, and reckless. Addie had dark hair, serious brown eyes, and a careful, quiet way about her. Eleanor liked to play practical jokes.

Once, under her direction, Addie had carried a harmless brown bull snake on the end of a stick and put it under a pile of her classmates' sunbonnets. She felt guilty but managed to keep a straight, solemn face as their victims shrieked, and the sunbonnets slithered away. Eleanor, on the other hand, laughed long and loud.

She seemed fascinated by what frightened Addie. Eleanor delighted in frogs leaping from lunch pails, wild electrical storms, and Fourth of July fireworks. Addie did not enjoy bad weather, loud explosions, or surprises with her bread-and-butter sandwiches. She preferred reading or playing pretend games, like floating pirate ships made of sticks down the creek or hunting for elves and fairies and enchanted buried treasure in the woods near their farm. But she was always willing to help when Eleanor announced she had what she called "a magnificent, new, wonderful idea."

Eleanor was starting her third year this fall at the brick schoolhouse that had just been built in Sabula, the town nearest their farm. The schoolhouse was a mile away. Each family who lived nearby paid for their children to attend. Last year was the first time Pa had had enough spare money to send Addie. If she were still home, she'd be at the new schoolhouse, too, learning to write in cursive with a pen and a real bottle of ink. Where they were going in

Dakota, there weren't any brick schoolhouses, her mother had said. More book learning would have to wait. But Addie did not want to wait. She liked school. She didn't want to have to go to Dakota, so far away from school and Eleanor and all her magnificent, new, wonderful ideas.

When Addie had told Eleanor that she was moving to Dakota, Eleanor at first refused to believe her. "Addie Mills, that can't be true. You wouldn't last a minute in Dakota Territory. Ma says it's all blizzards and grasshoppers and hot and dry as a desert only worse. You're just not a sodbusting pioneer-type."

After a few days, Eleanor had apologized to Addie for saying she wasn't a pioneer-type. But Eleanor's words somehow stayed inside Addie's head. Maybe she really didn't have what it took to live in Dakota.

"Addie Mills!" her brother George cried. "Addie! Addie!"

"Addie! Addie!" the grass answered.

Still Addie said nothing. She was tired of stepping over the sharp stubble of dry ripgut and thistles, of moving on and on behind the wagons with eight-year-old George and four-year-old Lew. The Mills family had begun traveling in early September. Almost six rainless weeks had passed since Addie had seen the Mississippi River bluffs near Sabula in eastern Iowa. Because they were using oxen to pull one wagon, they sometimes made only eleven miles a day. It was nearly five hundred miles from Sabula to their homestead in Dakota. Now they had only four or five days' travel left ahead, but those days seemed like forever.

Sometimes when her legs began to ache and her feet were sore, she'd climb up next to her father on the wagon seat. If George was already there, smiling at her with one of his nasty smirks, she'd have to listen to him and Pa telling stories about how much better their new farm in Dakota would be. It made Addie jealous to see Pa and George together, talking and laughing as if this were an exciting adventure instead of a long, tiring trip away from everything familiar.

There was no one to really talk to. If she went inside the wagon, she had to watch her two-year-old brother, Burton Grant. Burt sat unhappily on a pile of bedding. He was still too young to be trusted to walk beside the wagon. He might fall under a moving wagon wheel or wander away and get lost.

"Play with me," he'd beg. But Burt was too little to talk to, and besides, it was too noisy in the wagon. Addie's seven-week-old baby sister, Nellie May, cried and cried from the colic.

Mother was so busy taking care of the baby, setting up their camp each evening, and making sure Lew and

Burt didn't tumble into the fire or crawl under a horse that she and Addie scarcely had time to talk the way they used to back home. "Becca, why don't you go inside and lie down a spell?" Pa told her almost every day, opening the wagon flap for her to crawl inside. Mother would tenderly cover sleeping Nellie May and gratefully curl beside her on the feather quilt for a nap.

It made Addie worry to see her so tired. Back in Iowa Mother always sang and sang. Since they had started out on their journey to the Dakota Territory, she was always quiet and sad. Mother told Addie she was especially tired after the baby was born. Nellie May was the reason they waited until September to leave for Dakota. Because of Nellie May, Addie had to do more than her fair share of chores, including building the fire every morning and helping with the cooking.

Addie knew Mother had not wanted to make this trip, either. It was hard for her to leave behind her father and all her sisters, cousins, and friends. The day they left Sabula she had told Aunt Ida she doubted she'd see any of the Iowa family again. "You may be the last civilized woman I'll ever set eyes on," Mother had said. She was certain there'd be no more church socials, quilting groups, county fairs, or big Fourth of July picnics with brass bands and firecrackers.

In Maquoketa, a town just thirty miles from Sabula, they already had electric lights and paved streets downtown. "There won't be anything as fine as Maquoketa near our claim, Rebecca," Pa had told Mother. "But there's Scotland, a town only fifteen miles from Oak Hollow that's growing by leaps and bounds."

Mother had smiled half-heartedly when she heard this. She seemed doubtful that they'd ever find anything in Dakota as civilized as what they'd left behind in Jackson County.

"Samuel, I know Dakota's our best chance to finally own our own land, but I can't help thinking about the dangers. They say Dakota's part of the Great American Desert. Wherever will we get our water? And what about the Indians? What about the blizzards?"

Pa had tried to reassure Mother. "Now, Becca, stop fretting. When I picked out our claim at Oak Hollow this summer, I never saw more beautiful land in all my life. It was as green as green can be. As for the Indians, the ones I met were all peaceful folk from the Yankton Reservation. We'll have a house built so snug we won't have to worry about any Dakota blizzard."

Addie remained unconvinced. Dakota looked anything but green. The grass was faded yellow and bronze. Most of the creeks they had crossed were nothing but dry paths through peach willows. There had always been plenty of water in Sabula, the sleepy little town by the shining Mississippi. She missed Grandpa and her cousins and all the secret places she played in on their farm. Addie could not understand why Pa believed Dakota was their last, best hope.

"Addie, come on out! We're leaving!" George shouted. He was a year and a half younger than Addie, but he was always telling her what to do. "If you stay here, the Indians will get you."

Addie caught her breath. Since they'd crossed the Big Sioux River, they hadn't seen one Indian. But that's all her brothers liked to talk about. Indians. How they scalped homesteaders and tied children to ponies and rode away with them as captives. Twenty-one years earlier, during the Minnesota Outbreak, hundreds of homesteaders in Minnesota had been massacred by angry Sioux. Even though the year was now 1883, people back home in Iowa talked about the terrible killings as if they had happened only yesterday.

The Mills's homestead in Dakota would be only a mile from the Yankton Indian Reservation! Pa said he chose the claim because it was the best land he could find still open for homesteading. "What with the speculators buying up land and the government giving away even more to the railroads, we're lucky I found what I did," Pa had told them. "And the Yankton Reservation Indians won't cause any problems. They're farming their own land now. I even heard the government's building them a school on the reservation."

Somehow Pa's words didn't reassure Addie. Eleanor had told her that seven years ago at Little Bighorn an entire company of U.S. Cavalry had been wiped out by Sitting Bull and his braves. How could her father be certain the Indians who lived so close wouldn't also become angry?

"Addie!" George cried. This time his voice sounded different. There was something frantic and fearful in George's yell.

"I'm coming!" Addie called. George was standing completely still, staring at something on the ground.

"It's a rattler, Addie," George whispered. His dark eyes were wide with terror, and his brown curly hair was matted with perspiration against his pale face. "Help me."

Addie gulped. She looked down in the grass and was relieved to see nothing but a harmless bull snake. It had a stout, brown, five-foot-long body like the snake she had carried for Eleanor. Quickly, she picked up a rock and hurled it. In an instant the hissing, pointy-headed reptile disappeared in the grass.

"That wasn't any rattler, George. It was just an old bull snake." Addie laughed. "He only eats rats and mice. And cowards."

George's pale face flushed pink. "I knew it was a dumb bull snake," he said and took off in a wild gallop toward the wagons.

"Where have you been?" Pa called to Addie. "We're loading up."

Ed and Will, their bachelor neighbors from Jackson County, had already harnessed the team of horses to the wagon they shared. The other two wagons belonged to Addie's family. One was filled with bedding, clothing, and cooking equipment for the trip. The second was filled with supplies for the new homestead. Ed and Will took turns driving the Mills family's second wagon.

Addie watched Ed smother the fire Will had made from buffalo chips, dried buffalo manure. Addie and George had gathered the chips near their camp last night. The manure made a good smokeless fire.

"What are you staring at, little missy? Ain't you got some jobs that need tending?" Ed winked at her. "Time's a-wasting."

Addie smiled at Ed, who had bright red hair and never went anywhere without a chew of tobacco. Will, on the other hand, neither chewed nor spit. He amused himself

and Addie during the long days of traveling by playing a harmonica.

Addie rubbed the tin cups and plates with a little sand to clean them. Water was precious and had to be saved for drinking and cooking. She put the dishes in a canvas bag and handed this to Mother, who was packing a kettle and a coffeepot into the back of the lead wagon. Carefully Mother covered the bucket of milk from Big Jones, their red milk cow. They would use the milk later that evening in their dinner gruel.

In Sabula Addie had watched Mother and Pa gather and load all the supplies they'd need to start a new home in Dakota. There was a barrel filled with a teakettle, an iron bake oven, an iron spider or frying pan with legs, and a coffee grinder. Hanging on the outside of the second wagon was a water keg, a polished steel breaking plow, a crate of Mother's chickens, and an extra set of harnesses. Inside were three bags of seed, a bag of potato cuttings, a butter churn, a washtub, a scrub board, a small cookstove, and a wooden box of home remedies. Mother had packed bandages, quinine for malarial fever, and morphine for pain.

Bedding was stored in the first wagon in tight rolls that unfolded easily when night came. During the day they could sit on the rolls as the wagon moved along. All the clothing they weren't wearing was carefully packed in a large steamship trunk. Wrapped in newspaper at the bottom were photographs of family and friends they had left behind. Even the thought of those pictures made Addie more homesick.

Pa threw an extra shovelful of dirt on the fire to make sure it was out. No one could take any chances of leaving even one spark alive. This was a dangerous time of year to travel. Throughout the long, wet spring and summer, the prairie grass had grown lush and thick. During the rainless days of fall, the grass had become tinder-dry. A spark from a careless campfire or a bolt of lightning could cause the grass to explode into flames. Pa said it didn't matter that the night air was sometimes so cold that frost covered the ground when they awoke. A prairie fire could start any time. With a wind behind it, a fire blizzard could race as fast as a horse could gallop, burning everything in its path.

If a fire broke out and the covered wagons couldn't make it to a river or creek in time, Pa, Ed, and Will would try to make a firebreak. The wagons and livestock would be gathered together in the center while the men carefully burned a strip of grass in a circle around them. It would be this strip of charred grass that would save them. "A fire can't go where there's nothing to burn," Pa said. "But if the wind is too strong, even a firebreak won't work. Then our only hope would be to set a backfire and keep well inside a cleared area of charred ground."

Addie hoped they wouldn't have to use this plan. She couldn't understand how starting another fire to meet an oncoming fire blizzard would save them.

Pa frowned at Addie as they climbed into the wagon. "We've got to make eleven miles today," he told her. "We don't have time to go looking for you every time we're ready to get moving."

"Yes, sir," Addie mumbled. Her father was in a hurry. He had traveled out to Dakota earlier that summer to stake their claim, one hundred sixty acres in Oak Hollow Township, Hutchinson County, about one mile from the Yankton Indian Reservation, just east of the Missouri River. After they were settled, Pa planned to go to the U.S. Land Office in Yankton to file his claim. The law said the land wasn't yours until you began building on it. Until that time, he worried some other settler might jump title on his land. He hurried, too, because there would not be much time to stock provisions and build a sod house before the snow came.

Day after day, as the wagons crept slowly along, Pa's pale blue eyes never stopped moving, back and forth across the horizon, nervously searching for landmarks. His high forehead furrowed with lines of worry as he guided the oxen, searching the horizon for the grove of cottonwood trees that lined the James River. After crossing the Jim, as the river was called, they would have thirty-six miles to go to Chouteau Creek, then about twenty miles north to Oak Hollow. They would be only about fifty-six miles from their claim.

"How long? How long? How long till Dakota?" Lew asked Addie as they began following the slow-moving oxen again.

Addie shook her head. "I just don't care," she said tiredly, trying to remember what it had been like in Jackson County, Iowa, sleeping in a real bed with a real roof over her head.

## 2  LAND OF BEGIN AGAIN

Addie awoke to the sound of Canada geese flying south, their strange cries filling the cold morning air. During the past three days the Mills had traveled west more than thirty-six miles and were now looking for Chouteau Creek to follow north to Hutchinson County. Pa said they were only about twenty miles from their homestead. It was still nearly dark this morning, and the wind from the northwest reminded her of winter. Addie worried about what would happen to her family if they didn't get a house built before a blizzard set in. Will had told her stories about the Dakota Nor'westers that filled the sky with snow so fast travelers were unable to see. They became separated from each other and wandered lost until they froze to death.

"Smells like snow," Addie said to George, who dumped a pile of buffalo chips he had collected. Addie rubbed her hands together and pulled Mother's wool shawl around her shoulders to keep warm. She stirred the cornmeal mush that was their breakfast.

The children ate their mush slowly. Sweetened with sorghum syrup, the gruel didn't taste quite so bad this morning. Addie didn't like cornmeal mush when they ate it in Jackson County and she didn't like it now, but she knew this would be all there was to eat until they stopped to rest late that afternoon. Since they'd started on their journey, George and Pa had shot rabbits and prairie chickens to eat for dinner every now and then. The wild game was a welcome change from salt pork and jerked beef. But their usual fare was gruel with milk in the morning and gruel, fried salt pork, and biscuits for dinner.

"I could shoot a buffalo right between the eyes," George bragged, licking the back of his spoon.

"Could not. There aren't any more buffalo around here. Haven't been any for nearly a year. That's what Pa says," Addie replied and stirred the gruel in her bowl so hard it slopped on her apron. She knew the huge herds that had once roamed this part of the prairie were gone, wiped out by hunters who came with guns for hides or just for sport. Only bones, skulls, horns, and buffalo chips remained in the tall grass. "I bet I could get us some fresh game better than you could, with all your big talk."

George laughed and slapped his knee. "Pa isn't going to teach you to shoot. Mother says it's not ladylike for a girl to handle guns."

Addie felt her face flush. She wished her father would teach her how to use a gun. She wished George couldn't make her so angry all the time. "Hurry up and finish, Lew," Addie said brusquely, turning away from George's satisfied smile.

As the sun began to rise, Addie could see frost clinging to the delicate turkey-foot grass, another name for the big bluestem that grew in some places as tall as a man on horseback. The grass was called turkey-foot because its slender stem split at the end like a turkey's toes.

The dead-white needle grass in the distance already looked like snow. Most of the prairie flowers were only dried stalks with stripped seed heads. A few pods clung to frost-blighted stems. Once the last wild geese and cranes flew south, the prairie would be silent except for the "ti-ti-chu-ree" of snow buntings and the plaintive whistle of circling red-tailed hawks. These were among the few birds that braved winter on the prairie. Of course foxes, coyotes, prairie chickens, rabbits, and meadow mice had no choice but to stay.

"We don't have any choice, either," thought Addie. Someone else was living on the farm they had rented back in Jackson County, Iowa. It had been a hilly place with clay-filled soil where Addie's family had struggled to make a living for nearly ten years, ever since Addie was born. Pa had never had enough help to clear more of the bottom acres where the land was level and low and close to the Mississippi. He had used this part of the farm to graze what few cattle the family kept.

Three years ago the river had flooded their fields, washed away their small corn crop, and drowned every cow except Big Jones and Great Giant. The milk cows managed to escape because they grazed on a hill—they were too fat and lazy to walk all the way down to the bottom land. The flood covered the first floor of the house and knocked over the barn, floating it south. Addie and her family saved themselves by climbing the high bluffs nearby. They were just in time to see the bridge to Sabula snap in two from the force of wild, swirling brown floodwater. Woodchucks, rabbits, toads, frogs, and snakes— some half-alive, some drowned—had been washed up into the branches of trees. Addie had covered her ears to shut out the panic-stricken lowing of cattle desperate to find a place to stand up. Nearly fifty families in Jackson County lost everything they owned.

When the flooding was over, the Mills had two cows alive and their house still standing. Neighbors found Pa's Union Army papers in a tin box five miles downriver.

To help pay their debts, Mother had to sell her fancy wedding brooch, which she had hidden behind a fireplace brick before the flood. George and Addie and Mother milked Big Jones and Great Giant and churned nearly five hundred pounds of butter to sell in Sabula for cash. Two hungry winters followed. There never seemed enough to feed so many mouths.

It was the year after these bad winters that Pa decided to sell Great Giant, leave Jackson County, and homestead in Dakota. If they farmed one hundred sixty acres for five years, Pa said, the land would be theirs, free. They would never have to churn butter to pay a landlord again. For days Pa had spoken of nothing but Dakota.

"It is the Land of Begin Again," he told his family. "We can own our own land. It will be hard work, but it won't be any harder than staying here and starving. With the railroad going west, the whole prairie will be filled up before you know it."

Addie and George finished eating. "How will we know when we get to the homestead?" George asked Pa.

"We'll know because I'll remember. And I carved four hardwood stakes with our name at each corner of the claim," Pa replied. "Now, Addie, take this corn mush and some tea to your mother. She's in the wagon packing the bedding."

Addie dished up some gruel and poured a steaming cup of tea for her mother, taking care to sweeten it the way Mother liked.

"Mother?" Addie called into the quiet wagon, hoping that just the two of them could talk together alone. But as soon as she spoke, Nellie May awoke, crying.

"Addie, why did you wake the baby?" Mother asked crossly.

"I didn't mean to," Addie said quickly, handing breakfast to her mother. She was going to ask what would happen if they couldn't find their homestead's wood stakes because Indians had pulled them out of the ground. But she thought better of the idea and hurried away without saying anything at all.

It was another long day with nothing to see except more miles and miles of grass. Will said he was too tired to play his harmonica, so Addie and her brothers had to march alongside the wagon without music. When they grew tired of marching, they waved clouds of grasshoppers away with wands of Indian grass. All afternoon they wore crowns of dry sunflowers in their hair as they kept watch over the family cow.

"Don't let Big Jones wander away from the wagon like that!" George shouted to Addie as she and the cow searched a low bush for any remaining chokecherries. "Don't you know Indians like to steal cows?"

"I wish some Indians would steal *you*. Can't you think of anything else to do except give me orders?" Addie replied angrily. There were no chokecherries, and now she had thistles caught all over the back of her dress.

"Addie, do you really wish Indians would steal George?" Lew asked, his eyes wide with surprise. The idea seemed almost too horrible.

"I most certainly do. There's nothing I'd like better than to see George slung over the back of some wild Indian's pony." She knew she shouldn't say such awful things, but sometimes George made her so furious. What gave him the right to boss her around?

Suddenly, Pa stood up in the wagon seat and stared into the distance. What was it?

"Smoke!" he called out.

Addie gulped and ran to the wagon, scrambling up for a better look. Sure enough, beyond the next rise she could see a thin wisp of smoke.

"Ed, you hold my teams. I'll ride ahead and see what it is. If there are Indians camped, I'll be friendly. They won't do us any harm," Pa said. "If I find there's a fire loose in the brush, I'll shoot once into the air to signal you. If it's not bad, we'll try to put it out with sacks dipped in drinking water. But we may have to start a firebreak."

Addie waited nervously beside the wagon as she watched her father take his rifle and mount Ed's horse. She couldn't decide which would be worse, Indians or a prairie fire. It seemed like a long time before Pa reappeared. He was riding full gallop, waving his hat. His beard gleamed in the sunlight, and he was smiling. Addie breathed a sigh of relief. Everything was all right.

"It's a house ahead! A real soddy! The smoke's coming from the smokestack!" Pa laughed and called to Mother in the wagon, "Becca, there're some neighbors for you up ahead!"

Ed smiled and spit a wad of tobacco on the ground. "Maybe we can sleep with a roof over our heads tonight." Will yodeled and played up and down on his harmonica. Suddenly everyone seemed happy.

Addie gave George the cow's rope and climbed into the back of the wagon. This time she was careful to keep quiet. Mother was sitting up on one elbow, her wavy black hair hanging down her back in a loose braid. Addie hadn't realized before how dark the shadows were under her mother's brown eyes. Mother's face looked thin and pale.

"There are people in this lonesome place?" Mother asked. Addie nodded and sat down as the wagon lurched forward again. She wondered if the neighbors up ahead would be like those they had left back home. Sabula seemed like such a long time ago. Her sudden homesickness made her think of happier days, and she tried to remember the last time she had heard her mother sing. Nellie May tucked her tiny thumb into her mouth and closed her eyes. Addie thought the last time must have been before Nellie May was born. She looked at Nellie May's pink wrinkled face and bald head and wondered how such a tiny baby could be such a trouble. She couldn't help feeling jealous of all the attention Nellie May got. Burt crawled into Addie's lap and began to wind her long brown braid around his fingers. Having a new baby in the family had not been easy for him, either.

Mother said nothing to Addie. As they drew closer to the soddy, they could hear voices singing:

*Beulah Land,*
*sweet Beulah Land,*
*upon the highest rock I stand.*
*I look away across the sea*
*where mansions are prepared for me*
*and view the shining glory there,*
*my heavenly home forevermore.*

Upon hearing those familiar words, Mother burst into tears. Addie did not know what to do. It was the first time any of the children had ever seen their mother cry. Nellie May woke up and began to scream again. Burt hid his face in Addie's dirty apron. Stroking Burt's hair, Addie bit her lip and tried not to cry, but large tears rolled down her cheeks and landed in dark splotches on her brother's blond curls.

# 3 ADDIE MAKES A FRIEND

The face at the wagon flap startled Addie. She barely had time to wipe her cheeks and eyes. "Come on in, folks!" a red-faced woman said, as if there were absolutely nothing wrong. "The name's Fency. Anna Fency. But you can call me Anna. Mr. Fency, help these children down."

Another face appeared at the wagon flap. This time a gaunt-looking man peered in. "Good afternoon. You young ones look like you could scramble out of a patch of ripgut without much trouble."

Addie smiled a little, imagining how hard it would be to untangle herself from the thorny prairie grass. She, Burt, and Lew jumped to the ground.

"I'll be out in a minute," Mother called after them. "Please don't wait on me."

Mr. Fency was the tallest man Addie had ever met. The flat prairie must make him feel even taller, she thought, as he bent almost in half just to get a good look at her. "What's your name, little sister?" he asked.

"Addie," she replied quickly, feeling embarrassed to have made this giant man look so awkward.

"What about you fellows?"

Lew and Burt hid behind Addie. Only George spoke up. "That's Lewis and Burton Grant. I'm George Sidney Mills. I'm eight years old, and I can shoot a gun."

Mr. Fency's bushy eyebrows went up. "Ever shot an antelope?"

"Haven't seen one," George boasted, "but if I did, it would be dead meat in no time at all."

Mr. Fency threw his head back and laughed loudly. Addie wondered if he was poking fun at George. "Well then, maybe you and I can hunt up a couple of antelope steaks for dinner," Mr. Fency said.

George turned red but was obviously pleased. He looked even happier when Mr. Fency suggested that he help unharness the oxen and horses. "You look strong enough to carry a team's harness all by yourself," Mr. Fency said.

Addie peered about the Fency farm, hoping to find another little girl hiding someplace. A line of laundry flapped in the breeze. There were several sheets, three pairs of overalls, a large apron, and two pairs of underwear made from flour sacks with the labels "Prairie Lily" and "Platte Peerless" still showing, but no small girl's clothes.

She sighed with disappointment. It seemed that the only people who lived here were Anna and Mr. Fency.

"A hired man helped me break nearly fifteen acres last spring," Mr. Fency told Pa proudly. "There is the firebreak we plowed around the house and this here is the lean-to for the cows. That's quite a bit of work done, considering we've only been homesteading since last fall."

Pa nodded and looked impressed. Addie wondered what her father saw. The Fencys had no fences built and no pigs. A few chickens scratched around the packed, bare ground in front of the soddy. The outhouse was nothing but three walls of sod. It had no roof. She wondered what the Fencys did when it rained.

From a distance, all the soddies she had seen on their journey looked like sleeping animals crouching on the prairie, their roofs covered with furlike tufts of dried grass and sunflower stalks. Up close the Fency soddy didn't look like an animal, but more like part of a hill. Only the tin stovepipe coming out of the roof made the structure resemble a real house.

Addie had always lived in a frame house with a plank floor and an upstairs and a downstairs. She didn't like the idea of living in a dirt home with just one window.

Behind the house Mr. Fency showed Pa the beginning of a well. The mouth was circled by a row of sod bricks, hastily piled in place. "So we don't fall down in there in the middle of the night," Mr. Fency explained. He and his hired man had dug for almost eleven feet before reaching water. They had not yet finished siding the well with stone. There was three feet of water down there now, and Mr. Fency hoped to dig the well deeper in the spring. A bucket tied to a long rope was lowered to bring up water.

"The creek nearby completely dried up by early fall," Mr. Fency told Pa. "The nearest running water's a river two miles from here—a long walk every day for drinking water. We had no choice but to dig a well."

"It must have been a lot of work," Pa said.

"It was," Mr. Fency agreed. "But the real heavy job was building the soddy. We couldn't have done it without the hired fellow. Would you like a tour?"

"Certainly," Pa said in good humor. He called to the children, "Come inside with us! It's a real soddy, just like the one we'll build when we get to Oak Hollow."

Addie touched the soddy's wall and outlined with her finger one of the big sod bricks that was nearly eighteen inches long. The bricks had been cut from the earth and were carefully laid in rows, one layer atop the next, to form walls. The walls rose up around a wooden frame that held the house's only window, which was covered with a piece of canvas from the Fencys' covered wagon.

Even the roof was made of dirt. Addie walked all the way around the house. It wasn't much bigger than two cowstalls in Grandpa's barn back home!

She gingerly pushed aside the piece of canvas that hung over the doorway, letting in a shaft of light. "Why, there isn't even a real wooden door," she thought. Because she had been standing out in the bright afternoon sunlight, the inside of the soddy seemed pitch black at first. The window let in a glimmer of light when the canvas blew in the wind.

Anna bustled into the soddy and pushed back the canvas door flap completely, so that the little house was suddenly filled with sunshine. In the middle of one wall Addie could see a cast-iron cookstove with four cook holes on top. There was a crude wooden table, a large trunk, and several wooden crates and nail kegs. Next to the stove was a cupboard filled with a few pots and pans, tin cups, forks, and spoons. Against another wall was a wooden bed frame with a feather tick.

"It's not what you call spacious, but it's home. Next spring Mr. Fency said he'd get me a sack of lime from town so I can whitewash the walls. Won't that look bright and pretty?" Anna announced, her hands on her wide hips. Her grey hair was gathered behind her head in a tight bun that made her flushed face appear even rounder.

Addie stepped inside. She immediately noticed that the soddy didn't smell like any house she had ever been in before. Maybe it was the dirt walls or the dried grass spread on the hard-packed dirt floor. The odor reminded her of the inside of an old haystack after a rain.

"Good afternoon," Addie heard a familiar voice say. She spun around to see her mother carrying Nellie May all bundled up in their best quilt. Mother was wearing a clean apron, and something else about her looked different. Addie realized it was her hair, which had been combed neatly and pinned into a bun, like the one Anna wore. "It is very kind of you to let us spend the night," Mother said quietly.

"It is our privilege. We always welcome visitors. And I do hunger sometimes to see young faces. May I?" Anna smiled, holding out her arms to cradle sleeping Nellie May. Mother blushed and handed her the baby. "Look at those tiny hands! Mr. Fency says I'm sentimental when it comes to babies. It's because none of ours lived, I guess. Please sit down while I put on a fresh pot of coffee."

"Well, if Anna Fency'd like, she's welcome to keep that baby. All it ever does is scream," thought Addie, noticing her mother was smiling.

"Addie," said Mother, "will you take Lew and Burt outside to play while Mrs. Fency and I visit?"

Addie nodded grimly and dragged her two brothers outside. She didn't want to go just yet. She would have rather stayed with Mother since she seemed to be in such an unusually good mood.

"Don't play near that well," Anna called. "It's not finished."

Addie and the two boys walked out to the firebreak and poked their toes in the bare, charred ground.

"Fire!" Lew shouted, marching along the strip of blackened earth.

"Hot! Hot!" chanted Burt.

Addie sighed and watched her father and Mr. Fency standing in the plowed field. They were poking a long stick into the ground. Mr. Fency pulled it out and showed Pa a black mark indicating just how deep the farm's topsoil was. On the next rise Addie could see George with Ed and Will. They had taken the horses and cattle out to graze. She imagined them talking and laughing together. It seemed as though everyone had a friend but her.

"Look!" shouted Lew, pulling a piece of bleached buffalo bone from the grass. He handed the bone to Addie. She turned it over and over in her hands. The bone was not much larger than the length of her arm from her elbow to her wrist. It was smooth and bleached perfectly white, with one end wider and rounder than the other.

Addie had an idea. She found a piece of charred stick from the firebreak and used it to draw a face on the bone. It was a little girl's face with long eyelashes and a large smile. Her brothers laughed and clapped when she showed them what she had done.

"Now all we need is hair," she said. "Come on, let's find some goldenrod."

The three children tramped along through the dry grass single file. "Here!" shouted Lew, running to his sister with a handful of the faded, downy tufts. Addie took off her apron. She placed the fluff on one end of the bone and carefully wrapped the cloth apron around and around to hold the new doll's hair in place. To make sure the goldenrod would not slip, she needed to fasten the apron securely. But how? She found a long root and tied it around the doll's neck.

"Isn't she stylish?" Addie said happily. "Burt and Lew, say hello to Eleanor."

Lew waved at the doll. But Burt had already lost interest and was wandering away.

"Eleanor, would you like to go with us for a walk?" Addie asked. She made the doll bow. "Then we will have a tea party."

"I don't like tea," Lew pouted. "Let's go make some poison chocolate with mud and sticks."

This sounded like an excellent idea to Burt, who followed his brother toward an empty creek bed a few yards away.

"Come back here, you two," Addie shouted. "What about Indians? You'll get kidnapped if you get lost!"

The boys stopped. They were looking at something on the ground.

"Now what are they up to?" Addie thought. "What if they really have found a rattlesnake?" She ran to the foot of the low rise where the two boys stood staring at the grass. There were three mounds, each marked with a clumsy wooden cross. Suddenly Addie thought of the cemetery behind the Methodist Church in Sabula. It was filled with crosses just like these. The mounds were graves. There were dead people under those markers! Maybe they had been scalped by Indians.

"Let's go now!" she said quickly and began hurrying Lew and Burt back toward the safety of the soddy.

# 4 DAKOTA BLIZZARD

Addie tucked Eleanor tightly under one arm and ran, holding each brother's hand as she dragged them along beside her. The children were breathless when they burst into the soddy.

"What's the matter?" Mother asked in alarm. She was holding Nellie May in her lap. For once, the baby was awake and not screaming.

"The three of you look as though you've seen a ghost," Anna said, pressing floury biscuit dough into a ball. The soddy was already filled with the smell of jackrabbit stew bubbling on the stove.

"We...we...found these graves. Down past the firebreak, near the dry creek bed. Whose are they? Were those people scalped?" Addie asked.

"Well now, why don't you sit down and rest yourselves?" Anna said quietly, pointing with her rolling pin at the feather tick. "I suppose I should start by saying last winter was one of the worst anybody can remember. From the end of October until almost March, there was a deep blanket of snow on the ground. Must have been nearly five or six feet. And wherever the wind blew, the snow drifted up ten feet or more. People from town said the drifts were higher than the telegraph lines along the railroad tracks that run east of Scotland. Luckily, we had enough food and fuel set by. Other first-year homesteaders weren't so lucky."

Addie glanced at her mother, whose face had suddenly become pale and emotionless.

"Now, there's a big difference between a snowstorm and a Dakota blizzard," Anna continued, rolling out the white biscuit dough with quick, expert strokes. "I remember one January day that started out sort of mild. But over in the northwest you could see a black bank of clouds rising over the horizon. Pretty quick the whole sky clouded over, and snow began to fall. At first it was light and white, filling the air like flocks of white snow buntings."

"Birds?" Lew asked, poking the dough with his fat finger.

"That's right, dear heart, birds." Anna laughed. "Then the storm came as if it were a wild animal let out of a sack. We were cut off from the whole world, surrounded by snow and wind. How can I describe that sound? It was like a shrieking and a low thunder. The whole house shook as if it were going to fly apart."

"How long did the blizzard last?" Mother asked.

"Three days. Three days of howling wind and blinding snow. It bit your face and eyes so badly you couldn't see your hand in front of you. Mr. Fency put up a rope between the house and lean-to so that he could feed the livestock."

"And what about those graves?" Addie asked.

"Well, I was getting to that part. On the second day we heard someone at the door. I couldn't believe anyone could be about. But a Norwegian who had just arrived and lived not far from here had come to us. He was nearly frozen and so caked with snow we could barely recognize him."

"Why did he come?" Addie asked.

"This is the sorrow of it," Anna said, dropping each biscuit from the cutter into a pan. "He and his wife and little girl lived in a claim shanty. It wasn't much more than tar paper and pine boards. They had just arrived and that's all they could build. When the Norsky realized we were going to have a true Nor'wester, he hitched his wagon and horse and decided to bring his wife and daughter to our soddy. He walked on foot, leading the horses and trying to keep to plowed ground to find his way. But unfortunately he dropped the reins of his team. And in that instant, the horses wandered off and were lost in the blinding storm.

"He searched and searched for them and somehow managed to make it to our door. He wanted to go back out there, to keep looking. Mr. Fency tried to convince him to stay with us, to wait until the snow cleared some. But he wouldn't listen. His English wasn't so good. Maybe he didn't understand. That Norsky just went back out there."

"What did you do then?" Addie asked.

"Mr. Fency tied a rope around his waist and attached it to the house. He went after him and stayed out until his feet were near frostbit. What with the cold and the wind so strong, Mr. Fency could barely walk. And the noise—I don't think that poor man could have heard Mr. Fency calling.

"Two days after the snow stopped, we found his body, just fifty yards from our house. We had to wait until spring and a thaw before we found his wife and little girl. We gave them each a regular, decent burial, even though we didn't even know their names. All we found in their shanty was a Bible with some queer, foreign writing on one page. They never had a chance to file on the land, so even the land office didn't know who they were or where we could send their belongings."

"How old was the little girl?" Addie asked. She had a sick feeling in her stomach.

"She wasn't much more than your age, I expect," Anna said quietly as she slipped the biscuits into the oven shelf to bake. "I'll never forget that father's face. Don't think Mr. Fency ever will, either."

The room was still. Addie tried to imagine what it must have felt like to have been that little girl, lost and cold, calling for her father to come back and find her. What if the same thing happened to them? What if Pa didn't get the soddy built soon enough?

Anna filled two big kettles with water from a bucket on the floor. "Now that I've got the stove good and hot, I'll put on some of the water Mr. Fency hauled by stoneboat from the river. It's nice clean water, not like the 'bug juice' we gather from ponds and sloughs after spring run-off. Then you can all have a nice hot bath before supper."

Anna slid the large wash boiler into one corner of the soddy. The boiler would serve as a bathtub. With help from Mother, she made a kind of curtain around the boiler by pinning a sheet to a rope. Addie carried buckets of water from the barrel outside that stood on the stoneboat, a sledlike, low platform used for heavy hauling. Boiling water was added slowly to the half-filled wash boiler.

"Ladies first," Anna said.

Mother took a bath, and then it was Addie's turn. After six weeks of dusty travel, she thought the warm water and lather from Anna's thick bar of homemade soap felt marvelous, even though the wash boiler was only big enough for her to sit in with her knees up. While Anna finished peeling potatoes and frying them with onions and lard, Addie and her mother washed Burt and Lew in the tub together.

"All right, gentlemen. You can dump the tub now and fill it up fresh. It's your turn," Anna called to the men.

Will and Pa carried the heavy tub outside and dumped it in Anna's garden. Then they refilled it with clean water and Anna added more boiling water from the kettles. Pa, Will, Ed, and George took their baths outside behind the soddy.

When everyone was finished, Anna pulled a second batch of biscuits from the oven and put the final touches on the stew. It was early evening, and even though it was the middle of October, the air was warm with a gentle wind blowing from the south. It was hard to believe that in a few weeks there could be drifts of snow.

Because the weather was so pleasant, Anna suggested they eat outside. Mother and Addie carried out the table and around it placed crates and kegs to be used as chairs.

At the foot of the Fencys' bed was a large, old trunk. There were leather straps and buckles on the outside and a worn rope handle at each end. The trunk's rounded top came nearly to Addie's waist. She watched curiously as Anna opened the lid and took out a linen cloth wrapped in tissue.

Anna carefully spread the cloth on the rough table and set out tin bowls, plates, and spoons. She flicked away flies with the end of a towel. "If this breeze keeps up, maybe the bugs won't bother us too much," she said happily as everyone sat down.

Her good stew of rabbit and turnips disappeared quickly. The potatoes and onions and tender biscuits soon vanished, too. For dessert, Mother brought out two jars of plums she and Addie had canned back in Sabula.

This was the first sit-down hot dinner the Mills family had had together since they left Jackson County. All their other meals had been eaten in shifts—adults first, children last—crouching around the smoky campfire or sitting inside the wagon if it was raining. George and Addie enjoyed their dinner too much even to give each other insulting looks.

"That was a fine meal, Mrs. Fency. Best biscuits I've had in a long time," Will said. "Ed is the only other person I know who bakes them as light."

Ed blushed bright red and pulled out a pouch of chewing tobacco. "I'd say I share that honor with Mrs. Mills."

"You're a man of many talents." Anna nodded at Ed approvingly. "I never believed that a bachelor's supposed to starve to death because he can't cook."

Offering Mr. Fency some of his highly treasured pipe tobacco, Pa cleared his throat the way he often did before making an important announcement. Addie put her spoon down and listened.

"I am grateful to the generosity of our new friends and neighbors for this fine meal," Pa said. "During our brief acquaintance I have happily discovered that, like myself, Mr. Fency is a veteran of the War of the Rebellion that pitted the North against the South. He served with distinction as an officer in the Twenty-fourth Michigan. I was only seventeen at the time I enlisted in the Thirtieth Wisconsin Volunteers, much to my mother's horror." Pa paused to smile at Mother and then raised his tin cup. "My family, my friends, and I thank you for your generosity. From one Union comrade to another."

Mr. Fency seemed touched and raised his tin cup in salute to Pa and then to Ed and Will, even though they were too young to have enlisted in the Union Army.

"I'd also like to thank Mr. and Mrs. Fency for allowing my family to stay with them for a few days. Because it is so important for us to get supplies as soon as possible so that we can begin building our soddy, Ed and Will and I are going to Scotland while the rest of the family stays here. We'll deliver the canned goods and lumber to our claim. By going alone, Ed and Will and I can cover ground more quickly."

"Pa, can't I come, too?" George pleaded. "I won't be in the way. And I can help you. I know how to use a gun."

"I want you to stay here to help Mr. Fency take care of the women and children," Pa said.

George looked terribly disappointed.

"Pa will return in two, maybe three days," Mother said. "Not long at all."

"Oak Hollow's only ten miles from here. From there it's eighteen miles to Scotland. We'll retrace our route back to the homestead with the supplies from Scotland. Then we'll return here. If we use the horses, we should be able to make good time," Pa added.

Addie was quick to notice that her mother did not seem at all upset about the idea of Pa's trip without them. And why should she? Mother and Anna were planning to go to the river to pick plums so that Mother could do some canning for the Fencys. They seemed to be enjoying their visit together. She heard Anna say that it might be months before the snow melted enough for another visit.

That night Addie and her brothers and Anna slept on coverlets on the floor. Mother and Nellie shared the bed, while Pa and the other men slept outside in the wagons.

For a long time, Addie lay awake. She listened to the sound of Lew snoring peacefully and the mournful tune Will played on his harmonica. It was warm and snug in the soddy, but somehow sleep would not come. She tucked Eleanor beneath her blanket and tried to recall the face of the real Eleanor, the best friend she had left behind. There was Eleanor, the hot summer night she and Addie had slept in the barn loft because it was too hot in the windowless attic bedroom.

The jump stories Eleanor had told about ghosts and ghouls frightened Addie so badly she'd threatened to leap from the barn loft into a haystack. Just before midnight they had put burlap oat sacks over their heads and crept into George's room. Days later she and Eleanor had laughed and laughed until tears ran down their faces, remembering how they had shocked George in the dark.

A tear suddenly rolled down Addie's cheek. How she missed Eleanor and their good times together!

Far away other creatures were crying. Wolves were howling again. Addie had first noticed their eerie, mournful sound when her family crossed the Big Sioux and entered Dakota. She sat up straight and listened hard, wondering how far away from the soddy they were. Pa was outside the door. He wouldn't let the wolves inside.

But the howling made Addie think of unpleasant things. If her father did not come back from Scotland, who would protect them? What if a blizzard began before they were able to build their own house and gather enough fuel? What if they became lost in the blizzard just like that poor Norwegian girl and her family?

When Addie finally dozed off, her sleep was fitful, and her dreams were filled with white birds.

## 5  LE

George stirred his oatm...
a pitcher of corn syrup...d him
to help Anna gather wha...tside
have left in the grass arou...night
brother was still angry abou... her
both upset that Pa, Ed, and...ere
bye. It was long before sun...od-
George was awake, that Pa h... or
empty wagon. He and Ed an...an
west. They planned on riding th...
to check on the family's claim...
squatter had built a house on th...
ride eighteen miles east to Scotl...
Scotland, it would be twenty-eight...
farm. As they traveled, Ed and Will...
unclaimed land was left in Hutchin...
found something that looked promisin...
own claims.

days. That's not long," Addie told

eanor secretly in her lap under the

*d another helping of side pork and*

enough," he replied, using his gruf-

-up voice.

will be able to come back for us?"

ad still not forgotten about what had

Norwegian family.

be not," George replied.

like her brother's answer. Was he trying

Or did he know something she didn't?

ou think he might not come back?" she

ewed slowly and swallowed. "Indians," he

Addie gave Eleanor a desperate squeeze. She

orrying so much about the weather that she

n about Indians. Pa had explained everything

eservation Sioux already—how they were peace-

hey were learning to farm. Still, Oak Hollow

a mile from the reservation. What if the Sioux

d there didn't like the idea of homesteaders so

hat if they were just hiding, ready to attack as

Pa returned to their land? What if—

"And that's why they should've taken me along," George said solemnly, wiping his sticky mouth with the back of his hand. "I know about Indians."

Now Addie was angry. George was just trying to scare her. "I don't believe a word of it, George Sidney Mills. You're a liar and a coward and that's the real truth."

George glared at his sister. "Pa said I'm in charge while he's away, so I'd mind my tongue if I were you."

"I'll mind it myself if you please," Addie said and stuck her tongue out at her brother. "Pa didn't take you along because you're a *coward*. Who'd want along a fraidycat who's even scared of a harmless bull snake?"

"And who'd want a dumb girl along who can't shoot or hunt or do anything except cry and cry all the time? 'Boo-hoo-hoo.'" George wailed menacingly.

If Mother weren't just outside, Addie knew she'd be in for real trouble. George hated to be called a coward more than anything. He hadn't forgotten about the bull snake he'd mistaken for a rattler.

"You're going to regret calling me a coward," George hissed at Addie as Mother returned with an armful of twisted hay. She placed a kettle of water on the stove to heat.

"What are you two quarreling about now?" Mother asked crossly. She opened the door to the cookstove and placed three tightly twisted knots of dry grass, called cats, into the fire. "There's chores to be done today, and I don't have time for arguments while your father's away. George, Mr. Fency needs help bringing up water for the cattle."

"Yes, ma'am," George said. He quickly stuffed the last of his pancakes into his mouth.

"Addie, you're going to help Anna and me with the washing. It's a good sunny day for drying, and Anna says she's got some nice soft rain water left in a barrel behind the house. It's better for washing than the hard well water. Who knows when we'll have another chance with winter coming? Now let's get moving. Anna has the washboard outside already. We've got nearly a month's laundry here."

"Yes, ma'am," Addie replied. Waiting until her mother's back was turned, Addie silently sounded out the word *coward* for her brother.

George stood up suddenly, knocking his plate to the floor. His face was fiery red.

"George! Didn't I tell you there's work to be done?" Mother said angrily.

Addie smiled sweetly at her brother.

"Yes, ma'am," George replied and quickly disappeared out the door.

"Don't know what's wrong with that boy," Mother muttered, gathering up the breakfast plates and handing them to Addie. Dipping the plates and cups into a precious bucket of water, Addie rinsed them clean and then used the same water to scrub the rough table. Anna said there hadn't been any rain here in more than two weeks. Until they finished the well, Anna said they needed to use water carefully.

Mother placed two clean muslin towels over the six loaves of bread she had baked earlier that morning. "We'll be needing plenty of cats twisted to finish the laundry. You and George and Lew can start now," she said. "There's dried grass piled outside the door. When that's gone, you'll have to go down by the creek bed to cut some more."

"Is Pa going to come back?" Addie spoke up suddenly.

"Of course, child." Mother laughed. "What makes you think he won't?"

Addie shrugged. She didn't want to tell her mother how much the story about the lost Norwegian girl had frightened her. Mother would think she was acting like a baby or, worse yet, like a coward. But her mother sensed something was wrong and knelt close, looking straight into Addie's eyes.

"Your father will come back, Lord willing. He's only going to be gone a short while," she said quietly. She brushed a piece of hair from Addie's troubled face and gave her a squeeze. "Seems I lean pretty hard on you these days, Addie. There's so much to do, and I've been so tired since Nellie May was born. I'm depending on you to be all grown-up so you can help me. Sometimes I forget you're still a little girl who needs a hug now and again."

Addie blinked hard and felt the corners of her mouth begin to quiver.

"Everything's going to be all right. Just look at Anna and Mr. Fency. Without any regular helpers like you or George, see how far they've come building a home and a farm here?"

Addie was still not persuaded. "It's not anything like our real farm back in Sabula," she said.

Mother smiled slowly. "You're right. It's not like Sabula. There's no Mississippi River to drown cattle or flood crops. There's no hilly land with poor soil. There's no scrub to clear away."

"And there're no woods," Addie paused and took a deep breath, "or Eleanor or Grandpa or Aunt Ida and the rest."

Mother sighed. "That's true. I know how hard it is to leave everyone behind. But we'll see all of them again one day. Mr. Fency told me there's a train now that runs clear across northern Iowa to Canton, Dakota Territory, and connects west as far as Scotland. Maybe in a few years, when we have a fine, big farm, we can send Eleanor a train ticket to come visit us. By then I bet we'll have a frame house built. Would you like that, Addie?"

"With an upstairs and a downstairs? Bigger than the one in Iowa?" Addie asked, warming up to the idea. She imagined Eleanor's look of amazement when she stepped off the wagon bringing her from the Scotland station and set eyes on the Mills's magnificent, new, wonderful farm.

"Maybe even with a parlor," Mother smiled. "Now go twist some more cats so I can get this water boiling."

As her mother stood up again, Addie suddenly gave her a hard hug. It had been a long time, long since before Nellie May came and they left for Dakota, that Addie had had Mother all to herself. She closed her eyes and did not want to let go.

"There you are!" Anna announced from the doorway. "I've got a second kettle going outside and some good lye soap I put up last fall. Addie, you'll help us, won't you?"

Addie nodded and wiped her eyes quickly so that George wouldn't guess she'd cried a little. Grabbing Eleanor, she ran out the door. She propped her doll against the side of the soddy and sat down. The sun was shining. She took a deep breath. She felt relieved that Mother seemed like her old self again. Maybe everything was going to be all right, just the way her mother had said.

Addie took a large clump of dry grass in her hand and twisted it into a hard knot. Lew and Burt were playing near the well. Addie could see them piling rocks all along the edge of the well wall. "You two stay away from there before you fall in. Come on over here and help me twist cats. I'll tell you a story."

Lew smiled and smeared the side of his face with his dirty hand. He and his brother loved to listen to Addie's stories, and she enjoyed telling them. It made work go faster. Eleanor always said she had a good imagination.

The two boys curled up in the dry grass and made cat noises, moving the hay cats up and down Addie's arm as if they were alive. "Once upon a time, there were two little boys named Burt and Lew," Addie began, working quickly as she spoke.

"Me!" Burt shouted.

"That's right," Addie said. "One day when they were walking over the prairie road, they saw a big cat. They followed that cat for many miles, up and down, up and down the little hills. Finally the cat stopped and said, 'Why do you follow me everywhere I go?' And Burt and Lew said, 'Because we want to get a better look at you.' But that wasn't the real reason. The real reason was that Burt and Lew wanted to play with the cat because they were so lonely on that big prairie.

"This was a magic cat and he already knew just what Burt and Lew were thinking. The cat said, 'Come with me and you won't be lonely anymore,' so Lew and Burt followed that cat to a magic Cat City. There were cats everywhere. They ran the stores and swept the sidewalks. They rode horses. There were cats in the jailhouse and cats in the big church."

Burt and Lew's eyes grew wide with amazement.

"'Well,' says the big cat to Lew and Burt, 'I'll make you both into cats. Then look at all the friends you'll have.' But Lew and Burt didn't know if they really wanted to have long tails and pointy ears.

"Then Lew asked, 'What do you eat in your Cat City?' And the big cat said, 'Mice and rats.' 'Mice and rats?' Lew and Burt asked. They didn't like that idea at all.

"'No, thank you, Mr. Cat,' they said and ran all the way home without ever stopping once. And do you know what they did as soon as they got home?"

"They ate chocolate wrapped in fancy papers!" Lew shouted.

Addie laughed. "You think that's what they ate, Burt?"

Burt nodded his head vigorously. "And what about you, Eleanor?" Addie asked, turning to the place where she had left her doll. But there was no Eleanor to be seen.

There was only her brother George leaning against the wall with a nasty smile on his face.

"How long have you been spying on me?" Addie demanded. "Where's Eleanor?"

"Cat ate her," George replied.

Addie was on her feet. "I put her here just a minute ago and now she's gone. Did you take her, George? Give her back, right now!"

"I didn't do nothing to her. Maybe the Indians got her. Maybe they scalped her," George said, grinning.

Addie ran all around the house, searching in the rain barrel, under the pile of twisted cats, behind the bucket near the well. Still smiling, George sat down and began twisting cats. She ran inside the soddy where Mother and Anna were loading the stove with more cats. Had they seen the doll?

"I don't think so—tell me what she looks like," Anna replied as she stood over the boiling tub of water on the stove, stirring sheets with a stick.

"She's not really a doll, you see. She's a bone I made into a doll. A buffalo bone. Oh, haven't you seen her?" Addie asked desperately.

Anna shook her head. Addie burst out of the soddy and ran to the lean-to, where Mr. Fency was piling up a wall of sod bricks.

"Mr. Fency, have you seen Eleanor?" Addie shouted.

"Who's Eleanor, little sister?" Mr. Fency asked, putting down his shovel and wiping his forehead.

"My doll. She's made of buffalo bone and my apron."

"Buffalo bone?"

Addie didn't like the way he was smiling, as if this were all some joke. "That's right. She's not very big. Only the size of my arm."

"Sorry, I haven't seen her. If I do, I'll be sure to tell you," Mr. Fency promised.

Addie ran back to Burt and Lew. Maybe they had seen what George had done with the doll. What if they hadn't? She'd tell her mother, that's what she'd do. Mother would make George tell what he'd done with Eleanor.

Lew and Burt were peering into the well.

"What are you two doing?" Addie yelled. "Didn't I tell you to stay away from there?" She hurried to the well and looked inside. The two boys were pulling on the rope that the Fencys used to lower the bucket for water. Something was floating down there. What was it?

Addie ran to the side of the house where she had seen Mr. Fency's ladder. It was nearly twice her size, but with all her strength she managed to drag it to the well. She tipped one end over the edge, and the ladder quickly fell in with a splash. It rested at the base of the well, the bottom rungs now covered with three feet of water. The top rung leaned against the well's inner wall. Addie did not hesitate for a moment. She had to save Eleanor. She swung her leg over the edge and felt a few feet down with her bare toe for the top rung. Slowly, she climbed down nine feet into the damp, dark coolness. When she looked up, the distance to the well's mouth was more than twice as tall as she was.

Bobbing in the murky water was what was left of Eleanor. Her face was gone. Her hair had floated away. She had been brutally scalped and left to drown.

Addie reached down from the ladder, scooped up the dripping remains, and cradled them in her arms. She knew the doll was gone forever. There was no making her better, no fixing her. She began crying softly. She would never forgive George for this—never.

As she climbed the ladder she could see Mother's angry face at the top of the well. "What do you think you're doing down there, young lady?" she demanded. "If your father were here, you'd get a licking. The well could have caved in on you."

"But, Mother—"

"You set a terrible example for your brothers. What if Burt tried to climb down there? Aren't you ashamed of yourself—"

Addie did not wait to hear her mother finish her sentence. Holding what was left of Eleanor tightly in her arms, she ran as fast as she could, past the cows, past George, past Mr. Fency. She leapt over prairie dog holes and through clumps of switch grass, her face flushed with rage.

## 6 ANNA'S GIFT

In a place George would never find, Addie buried Eleanor. She sat for a long time and looked at the spot she had decorated with bits of stone and tufts of dried butterfly milkweed. She wished she could have made a better wooden cross, but two sticks from a peach willow were all she could find. All around her the prairie grasses were faded and brittle. The land looked so sad, so empty. She hated to leave Eleanor in such a lonesome place.

When Addie stood up, she was surprised to see someone running toward her. Shielding her eyes from the sun, she recognized Anna.

"Are you all right?" Anna asked, out of breath, her face even redder than usual. "You scared us, child. Your mother and I have been looking everywhere for you. Your Ma's frantic with worry. You could get lost—you don't know your way around here. Why did you disappear like that?"

Addie clenched her teeth together. Why did grown-ups always demand reasons?

"I see you've been making a fancy funeral here," Anna continued, not really waiting for an answer. "Mighty nice decorations. You know, in late spring and summer, this whole prairie's as full of flowers as any garden could be. White and blue prairie phlox, ox-eye daisies, purple cone-flowers. Sometimes you can even find yellow lady's slippers or moccasin-flowers in the marshy places. Rose-purple blazing star, that's one of my favorites. All of them more beautiful than any you'd find in a big-city funeral."

Addie still said nothing. It was hard to imagine anything beautiful growing in Dakota. Besides, right now what did she care about prairie wildflowers?

"George killed my doll. I buried her."

"Is that why you ran away?" Anna asked.

"Mother didn't even give me a chance to tell what George did to Eleanor," Addie said bitterly.

"What George did was wrong," Anna agreed. "But I think your mother was frightened when she saw you climb out of that well. You scared her pretty bad. That well's not finished yet, and it could have collapsed."

Addie stuck out her chin. "I wish it had. I hate this ugly place. There's nothing here. It's empty. I never wanted to leave Iowa."

Anna put her arm around Addie. "You know, it's a funny thing about the prairie. It isn't pretty the way most people use the word. But sometimes in the middle of the afternoon, I'll be out tending my garden and I'll stand up in the bright sunshine and look out at all those miles and miles of grassland with the shadows of clouds galloping past. And suddenly I feel this freedom. Just me and the sky and the land. I'm completely happy. It's not like anything you feel in the middle of a city or in a forest. There's a vastness here that swallows you up and lets you go all at the same time."

Addie was puzzled, but she tried to understand what Anna meant. "But I feel so afraid here. We didn't have any Indians near Sabula or wolves howling all night or blizzards that kept you from seeing neighbors days on end. I'm not the sodbusting pioneer-type, I guess. And I feel so lonesome all the time."

"Let me tell you a little secret. When I first came here, I was frightened and discouraged, too. But little by little as Mr. Fency and I began working—breaking the land and building a house and planting my kitchen garden—I began to see this place as my new home.

"Sometimes I feel lonesome, too. But as more and more people come out here and settle like we're doing, the less lonely it'll be. Look at us. You and I are friends. Mr.

Fency and I are awfully fond of you and your Ma and Pa, your brothers, and your baby sister. Your family loves and cares about you, too.

"As soon as you get to Oak Hollow and start to work on your new homestead, you'll feel better about Dakota. There's something special about working your own land and building your own farm. You'll see."

"I'll never get any book learning now. There aren't any schools here."

"Well, I've heard that Hutchinson County's filling up so quickly, they're already talking about a schoolhouse," Anna said. "In the meantime, I can help. I have some books in my trunk I brought all the way from Michigan."

"You do? Real books?" Addie asked. "Mother knows how to read, and so does Pa. But we just never had enough money to buy any books. Would you really let me use yours? I promise to be careful."

"Of course," Anna laughed. "We have *Aesop's Fables*, an old school primer, and the Bible. You can read them anytime you want. Now, come along with me. I think I have something else that will help you. Something very special."

Addie held Anna's hand all the way back to the soddy. They passed Mr. Fency backsetting ground he'd broken earlier that summer. The Fency horses strained, pulling the polished steel breaking plow. It left behind a clean black ribbon of sod. Rain and snow and wind would break down the grassy, root-filled sod clumps over the coming winter, making it easier to plow again and plant in spring.

"Now, come here so you can see," said Anna as they entered the soddy. Carefully she lifted the lid of the trunk where she kept the linen tablecloth. Addie was amazed to see how many things Anna had stored inside the trunk, which smelled strongly of camphor. She pulled out several bundles, a folded blanket, a winter coat, and a giant pair of boots. She handed Addie three books wrapped in newspaper. Addie fingered the gilt-edged pages of the Bible and marveled at the reader. But the last book seemed best of all. *Aesop's Fables* had beautiful colored pictures of people and animals that almost looked real.

"Oh!" Addie sighed, pressing her nose to the pages. "This book smells so delicious!"

Anna laughed. She rummaged deeper in the trunk. At the very bottom she found what she was looking for, something small covered in tissue paper.

"I was sure it was here somewhere among all my precious things," Anna said. "I've found it now. Addie, this is for you."

Addie pulled the paper away and found herself staring at two bright china eyes. They belonged to a doll with a painted china head and a body of soft, stuffed cotton. Her mouth was a perfect cupid's bow, and her hair was brown painted ringlets. The cheeks had a blush of color that made the doll's face look soft and real. She wore a long dress of red calico, the same kind grown-ups wore, and she was so small she fit easily in Addie's hand.

"She is beautiful," Addie whispered.

Anna smiled as she studied Addie's face. "I'm what Mr. Fency calls sentimental. I brought this doll all the way from Michigan. I've kept Ruby Lillian for a long, long time. You see, I always hoped I'd have a daughter. But it just wasn't to be. I buried three boy babies. But I've always kept Ruby Lillian. Well, she's yours now. I know you'll take good care of her."

"She has the most alive china face I've ever seen. Such tiny hands and feet! I never had a real doll before. I had to leave my cornhusk doll back in Iowa. Pa said we didn't have room for any toys on our way to Dakota."

"What will you call her?" Anna asked, carefully repacking the trunk.

"Ruby Lillian, of course," Addie said. "It's a beautiful name." She placed Ruby Lillian deep in her apron pocket where she would be safe. "Do you think my mother will make me give her back?" She could hardly believe anything so lovely could be hers.

"No, I don't. Ruby's my gift to you. I bet your ma had a doll just like her once."

"That's right." Mother stood in the doorway of the soddy. Her face was flushed and wisps of hair from her bun had come undone. "Your grandpa bought a china-head doll for me in Sabula when I was a little girl." Tiredly, Mother sat down on the edge of the bed and took Addie's hand. "Why did you run away like that? I've been looking everywhere for you."

"I found Addie down past the creek bed. She was saying goodbye to someone special," Anna said quietly, closing the trunk. "We had a little talk. Woman to woman. Addie's going to take care of Ruby Lillian for me now."

Addie took the doll out of her pocket and showed it to Mother. "I promise not to scare you like that again, Mother," she said slowly. "It's just that George—"

"I know now what George did," Mother interrupted. "Lew told me. And I'm sorry I shouted at you like that. But crawling into that well was a very dangerous thing to do. And I depend on you to set a good example."

"I'm sure Addie won't go down there again," Anna said.

Addie turned Ruby Lillian over in her hand. "Can I keep her, Mother?"

"If it's all right with Anna, it's all right with me."

"And you won't tell George?" Addie asked.

"Absolutely not," Mother promised.

"Ruby Lillian will be our secret," Anna whispered and grinned.

"Thank you, Anna." Addie smiled and put the doll carefully back into her pocket. That evening at dinner, she didn't notice when George tried to get her attention by secretly making grotesque faces over his fried cornmeal mush and molasses. She didn't even become upset when he asked her how Eleanor was feeling. Addie just smiled and smiled with her hand in her pocket. With her thumb she could feel the cool china features of Ruby Lillian's tiny face.

# 7 INDIANS!

The time Pa was gone passed quickly for Addie. The weather was warm and sunny with no signs of rain clouds anywhere on the horizon. When the wind blew, the expanse of dry grass on all sides of the Fencys' farm rippled the way Addie remembered the wide Mississippi River moved in the wind.

Mother and Anna cleaned all the Mills's bed ticks. First they emptied the old straw from the big cloth cases, which were then washed and dried. Then each clean tick was filled with bright, fresh straw through a hole which unbuttoned in the case's center. The mattresses would not be cleaned and restuffed for another year.

Addie helped Mother and Anna slice cabbage heads from Anna's garden, place the chunks of cabbage into jars, and fill the jars with brine. "Now we'll have cabbage to eat all winter," Anna said when they were done.

There was so much to do Addie scarcely had time to worry about Pa. After she'd finished all her chores, she liked to climb up the ladder with Ruby Lillian and sit on the gently sloped soddy roof. Anna had told her that Mr. Fency built the soddy so well a grown man could dance up there and no one inside would hear him.

The roof was Addie's special place away from her brothers. Without anyone to bother or tease her, she built Ruby Lillian her own little sod house, complete with a little tea set made of bits of hollow seed pods and leaves. She made her doll beautiful cakes of mud and grass mixed with water. Addie liked to play school with Ruby Lillian, too, teaching her how to draw the letters A, B, and C in smoothed dirt.

The secret tea parties and school lessons never lasted long. There were always more chores to do, always more buckets of water to carry or cats of dry grass to twist. Mother and Anna were cleaning and cooking as fast as they could to get everything ready for the winter ahead.

"Addie!" Mother called one afternoon. "Come down and watch your brothers!" Addie quickly hid Ruby Lillian in her pocket until the next time they could be alone. "Anna, George, Nellie May, and I are taking the wagon down to the river to look for the last of the wild plums. Mr. Fency is going with us, to cut sloughgrass. I want you to keep your eye on Burt and Lew while we're gone. They're both napping now. If you're lucky, we'll be back before they wake up."

Addie was disappointed she couldn't go along. But being out from under the watchful eye of George meant she and Ruby Lillian could finish their school lesson.

"We'll be back before you know it!" Anna shouted from the Fencys' wagon as it pulled away.

"Remember, stay away from that well!" Mother called. Addie waved goodbye as the wagon passed beyond the blackened firebreak encircling the sod house. Then she climbed back on the roof.

The wagon disappeared over the next rise in the prairie and was gone. Scanning the horizon, she was reminded again that there was no sign of neighbors in any direction. If there were just one barn roof, one smoky chimney pipe visible, she knew she wouldn't feel so completely alone. "An afternoon's not long," Addie reassured Ruby Lillian, as she began their lesson again.

When they were through studying, Addie poured imaginary tea into milkweed-pod teacups. Suddenly she felt as if someone were watching her. But how could that be? The others were nearly three miles away. In all directions she could see nothing but prairie grass moving in the wind. The sky above looked more enormous than ever.

"I'll go see if Burt and Lew are awake yet," Addie said to herself, climbing down the ladder and hurrying into the soddy. She felt safer there. Lew and Burt still lay snoring, curled up together on the bed like two little prairie dogs in a burrow. Burt's blond curls were all she could see above the top of the quilt. Addie touched his hair. He was the only child in the family with hair that color. Lew, Addie, and George all had brown hair. Sometimes, in the right light, it seemed to Addie as if Burt's hair glowed.

She peeked under a piece of cloth on the table. Anna had left behind an entire pan of corn bread for them in case they got hungry. There was far more than three children could eat in one afternoon. Twisted cats were piled next to the stove, and on top a pot of beans for supper bubbled gently.

After checking her brothers, Addie decided to go outside and make sure nothing was prowling around Anna's chickens. Bess and Missy, the Fencys' two milk cows, and Big Jones were picketed on a long rope inside the firebreak. She patted Big Jones and was about to give her an extra helping of grass when she saw a tall shape—a person—dart around the soddy.

Addie's heart began to pound. She ran back into the house, but Burt and Lew were still asleep. Nothing seemed to have been touched. She turned to pick up Ruby Lillian from the table where she had left her when again she felt eyes staring at her. This time she knew it was not just her imagination. She whirled around in time to see a brown face and a pair of deep black eyes disappear from behind the canvas flap at the window.

Indians! Real Indians!

George had once told her that Indians loved to scalp boys with curly yellow hair and girls with long brown braids. Addie shivered, remembering his words. Quickly she threw a quilt over her sleeping brothers to hide them and put on her sunbonnet, tucking her long, brown braid inside where it couldn't be seen, just in case what George had said was true. She dragged the heavy table across the floor to make a barricade in front of the doorway. But two dark shadows stood behind the canvas flap. It was too late.

"What do you want?" she asked, her voice quivering. She stood in the doorway, determined not to move. She crossed her arms in front of herself to keep from shaking.

The two Indians wore leather leggings and faded blue long-sleeved cotton shirts. Each man's hair was long and hung down his back in a loose, glistening braid. Tall and powerfully built, they stood straight and proud before her.

"What do you want?" Addie asked again. Not far away she could see two Indian women. In spite of the warm weather, they wore blankets around their shoulders. Their hair was parted in the middle in two braids. The top of their heads where their hair was parted was painted red. The women didn't look angry or curious, only tired. One carried a papoose on her back, and Addie could see a tiny round brown face peering out. Nearby were two bony-looking dogs attached to two poles with a frame between piled with belongings.

One of the Indians reached out, as if to move Addie from the doorway.

"No!" her voice squeaked as she gripped the canvas.

The two Indians looked at her and then said something to each other and chuckled. Addie was surprised to hear them laugh. They sounded as though they found her amusing. She wished she could understand their words. There was something about the tallest visitor that seemed vaguely familiar. With a start, she realized his laughter reminded her of Ed when he chuckled at one of his own silly jokes.

Suddenly Addie felt someone pulling on the back of her dress. It was Burt! He was awake, and now he would be scalped, too. "Get back inside!" she hissed. Addie glanced inside the soddy and saw that Lew had climbed on the table. He was eating a large, sticky piece of corn bread smeared with molasses. Burt's face, too, was covered with the mess.

Spotting the two boys, the Indians made another motion with their hands. One Indian touched Addie's arm, then motioned to his mouth, again and again. What was he trying to show her? He pointed inside the soddy and made a movement toward his mouth again.

Suddenly Addie understood. The Indians were hungry. "Maybe they haven't come to hurt us at all," she thought. "Maybe they just want something to eat."

She ran inside the house and brought back the pan of corn bread. She broke off a large piece to save for her brothers and gave the rest to the Indians, who sat on the ground and ate hungrily. They acted as though they hadn't eaten in a long, long time. She went back inside for a jar of molasses and poured some into a tin cup. When she handed the cup to the Indians, they used two fingers to quickly scoop the black sweet liquid into their mouths. When the cup was empty, they gestured that they wanted more.

When Addie ran inside to fill the cup again, she found a half loaf of bread her mother had wrapped in an old flour sack. She filled two bowls with beans and walked past the two men, who continued eating. The bread and beans she handed to the women. For the first time she saw them smile. Now that she was closer, Addie could see that the quiet papoose wasn't much bigger than Nellie May.

Carrying a baby on your back seemed much handier than having to tote a baby in your arms.

"What will I give them if they're still hungry?" she thought as she walked back to the soddy, where Burt and Lew stood curiously looking out.

"Don't crowd them while they're eating," Lew ordered his little brother.

Addie scooped two more bowls of beans and offered these to the men with a second cup of molasses. The Indian who reminded her of Ed looked up and smiled.

"You must be pretty hungry," Addie said. "Are you thirsty, too?" She filled two cups with a dipper of fresh water from the bucket near the stove. But when she came back outside again, the Indians were gone. Their bowls had been wiped clean and were stacked neatly by the soddy door. Next to the bowls was a necklace of delicate glass beads sewn on a strip of hide. Hanging from the necklace was one black-and-white eagle feather.

"See here, Burt and Lew. Look at this!" Addie said, smiling. "They left behind a necklace to pay for their food, same as Pa pays for supplies at the dry goods store."

Burt and Lew grinned. "Adda, Adda, ADDIE!" Burt shouted as his sister tied the necklace around her neck. Addie whirled around and around in the soddy. She wished Anna had a looking glass so that she could see herself.

"Maybe the necklace has Indian magic," Lew said.

Addie nodded. Maybe the necklace *was* magic. It was a wonderful surprise, but the biggest surprise was the Indians themselves. After all her fearful imagining, they were just people with troubles maybe not so different from her family's. Perhaps they were on their way to set up a new place to live before winter came, too.

Burt stuffed the last piece of corn bread in his mouth and reached up to touch the necklace with his sticky fingers.

"Isn't it beautiful?" Addie said, keeping the necklace just out of her brother's reach. "When George gets back we'll have to be sure and show him. He'll never believe we met real Indians!"

# 8 SURPRISES

"Look at me!" Addie shouted as Anna drove the wagon inside the firebreak. "I've got a real Indian necklace!"

"Where did you get that?" Anna asked.

"Four Indians and their baby came and left the necklace as payment. I gave them beans and corn bread. They were nearly starved. I didn't know what else to do."

"Indians? Are you all right? They didn't hurt you, did they?" Mother asked with concern as she climbed from the wagon with Nellie May.

"We're all fine. The Indians were just hungry, that's all," Addie said.

"Let me see that necklace, will you? I don't believe it's real," George said, his eyes narrowing for a closer look. "Addie's making it all up. I bet she just imagined the Indians so she wouldn't be in trouble for eating a whole pan of corn bread."

Mr. Fency examined the necklace. "Looks real enough to me. How would you describe the Indians?"

Addie took a deep breath. "They wore their hair in braids and the men wore blue shirts. They didn't speak English, so they talked to me using their hands. I understood what they meant after a while. At first I thought they wanted to scalp me and Lew and Burt, but then I figured out they were just hungry."

"I suppose they were reservation Indians, looking for some handouts. We've had them come here before. Never had any trouble. Sometimes they wander off the Yankton Reservation to dig wild turnips along the river banks when the government rations don't come in," Mr. Fency said. "They've got a hard life."

"You did the right thing to feed them," Mother said. "We have to learn to get along with the Indians now, since we're all going to be neighbors."

"Were you frightened, Addie? I know I was the first time the Indians came to call here," Anna asked, lifting a bushel basket from the wagon to take into the house.

Addie knew that George was waiting to hear her answer. "Oh, not at all," she said quickly. "I just stood right in the doorway, never once letting them into the house."

Anna winked at her. "That's my girl. Now let's go pit the plums we found. For dinner we'll make rice cooked with buttermilk—with some sorghum syrup on top."

"HOW!" George suddenly shouted, coming up behind Addie and startling her so, she jumped. He laughed and laughed when he saw how frightened she looked.

"You're just jealous, George Sidney! After all your big talk about Indians, you still haven't seen a real one."

"I am not. I still don't believe the Indians were even here. I think you made the whole thing up."

Addie folded her arms and took a deep breath. George was trying to make her upset, but she wouldn't give him that satisfaction. "I know what I saw and what I did. Everyone else believes me. I'm going inside now to help Mother," she said calmly.

Anna and Mother hadn't found many plums, but they were happy there were enough to can at least five jars. The fruit would be a welcome treat in the winter when there wasn't anything fresh. After helping pit the plums, Addie climbed to her favorite spot on the roof. Mother had given her one plum to eat. She closed her eyes and took a bite, enjoying its juicy sweetness. She wished she could tell someone else about the Indian visit. If only Eleanor were here! Addie imagined her coming across the prairie in a horse and wagon on her way from the train depot in Scotland. Wouldn't she be surprised when Addie told her how brave she'd been when the Indians came! Eleanor wouldn't dare call her fraidycat anymore.

The sun was setting, and the sky was beginning to fill with glowing clouds of pink and deep red and orange. She gazed into the horizon. Someone was coming. Maybe it *was* Eleanor. Addie stood up and began waving her sunbonnet in the air.

"Oh, look, Ruby Lillian. Eleanor sees us. She's waving back!" Addie cried, staring hard into the distance. Someone really was waving to her. As the small shape came closer, she could see that it wasn't Eleanor at all. It was a man driving a wagon, all alone.

"Mother!" Addie cried, hiding Ruby Lillian in her pocket and scrambling down the ladder. "Pa's coming! I see him, and he's all by himself!"

Her mother, brothers, Anna, and Mr. Fency ran out of the house and looked in the distance toward the next rise. Addie wanted to be the first one to greet Pa. She headed across the firebreak and through the tall grass, running so hard she was soon out of breath.

Her father helped her up into the wagon, which was empty except for a burlap sack in the back. "How's my Addie?" he asked, giving her a big kiss on the cheek. She was glad she had reached the wagon first. "What's that around your neck?"

"An Indian necklace. Four hungry Indians gave it to me for feeding them dinner all by myself." Breathlessly, she told Pa what had happened. "I was scared, Pa. But you know, those Indians were just like you said they'd be. They were just peaceful folks. They were looking for some food. I think they might have been trying to find a place to live before the snow comes, just like we are." Addie paused. "Pa, do you think I was awfully brave?"

Pa whistled in admiration. "I'd say you're probably the bravest gal in Hutchinson County."

"Really, Pa?" Addie asked, feeling proud and happy.

"I've heard only the bravest Indians are allowed to wear eagle feathers. Eagle feathers are very special. Now, if we were still in Sabula, I bet you never would have met real Indians or been given an Indian necklace for being kind and brave. Dakota's making you a right resourceful gal, Addie."

Addie smiled. "You really like Dakota, don't you, Pa?"

He nodded. "Anything's possible here, absolutely anything. Doesn't matter who you were before you came or how you did. That's what I like. We've got a chance to make good here, Addie. You and me and your ma and brothers and sister. We're here right at the start of something important—moving and building on land nobody's ever settled before. Doesn't that give you a good feeling?"

"I never figured it that way before," Addie replied. She sat close to Pa, listening to the sound the wagon made as it lurched along through the dry grass. What Pa said reminded her of things Anna had told her. Maybe one day she could think about Dakota the way Pa and Anna did. Up to now, she hadn't really thought about the new life they were starting. She had just been thinking about what they were leaving behind.

Pa interrupted her thoughts. "I've left most everything—the lumber, the canned goods—under a canvas tarp on the homestead of one of our new neighbors, just about a mile or so from our claim. Don't worry, they'll be safe."

"Say, Pa, where are Ed and Will? I thought they were coming back with you," Addie asked.

"They've made other plans. They decided Scotland was such an up-and-coming town, they're going to stay and work for the railroad. They'll make one dollar and seventy-five cents a day. By next summer they think they'll have enough money to buy land outright instead of working a claim for five years. Once they own land, the banks in Scotland will lend them the money they need to outfit themselves with plows and seed and maybe the lumber for a house."

"'But Pa, how will we build our own soddy if they don't help us?" Addie said with disappointment. She knew she was going to miss Ed's jokes and Will's harmonica.

"We'll manage somehow, Addie," Pa said. "Now, don't you fret. Cheer up. I bought you some surprises when I was in Scotland."

"Surprises?" Addie asked. "Real store surprises?"

"That's right," Pa said. But before he could tell her any more, her brothers and mother had stopped the wagon.

"How are you, Samuel? You look tired," Mother said as Pa kissed her. "What does the land look like? Is there anyone living nearby? And where are Ed and Will?"

"The claim's just as beautiful as I left it." Pa smiled. "Water's still running in Emmanuel Creek nearby. Our nearest neighbor's a man and his wife, name of Seaman. They have a fine herd of cattle."

"Do they have any children?" Addie asked.

"They've two grown sons. I didn't meet anyone else. But then again, I was only at their place long enough to unload our supplies. They're going to keep their eye on them until we get back."

"But what about Ed and Will?" Mother asked.

"Ed and Will decided to stay in Scotland to earn some money so they could buy their own land."

Mother looked worried. "But they were going to help us, Samuel. They promised."

"Don't worry now, Becca. Everything will be fine. We can build a soddy ourselves. You'll see."

That night after supper, Addie and George and Lew and Burt each received their own piece of rock candy, a clear lump of flavored, crystallized sugar on a string from the dry goods store in Scotland. Addie marveled at the rock candy's beauty. She held it up to the light by its string and twirled it around and around. It almost looked too beautiful to eat. She took three small licks and decided it was far more wonderful than even the sweetest wild plum. Carefully, she wrapped the candy in a corner of a clean handkerchief so that she could enjoy it again later. At three licks a day, it might last all the way until spring. Meanwhile Lew and Burt and George made loud crunching noises as their precious treats quickly disappeared. Addie tucked her wrapped candy inside her pocket. She wasn't going to take any chances that her brothers might still be hungry for more.

For supper Anna fried the salt pork and potatoes Pa had brought from Scotland. Addie decided everything tasted better because it came from a store.

"Scotland's even bigger than it was when I came through earlier," Pa said, leaning back against the soddy wall. "There's every kind of person there—rich folks, poor folks, young dandies from the East wearing fancy city clothes and shiny, pointy shoes, foreigners off the train wearing kerchiefs on their heads. There're Yankees,

Germans, Norskies, and Swedes, and I saw a whole lot of Russians. They have a part of town named just for them—Little Russia. I even saw a colored man get off the train. I tell you, I heard every kind of language. And of course there were Indians."

George's face lit up. "Indians?"

"Why, sure. They were everywhere, trading beadwork and pelts and wagon loads of buffalo bones for goods in the stores. The buffalo bones are shipped east to be made into fertilizer. The town's growing fast—there's more than one hundred businesses, they say."

"Sounds as if the place has been booming since we were there last, doesn't it, Mrs. Fency?" Mr. Fency said to Anna.

"There's a big Chicago, Milwaukee, and St. Paul train depot now with a horse-driven cab that takes rich folks to the fancy hotel, the Campbell House. I went inside just for a look." Pa winked at Mother. "There's a solid walnut staircase that goes up three stories."

"Three stories, my!" Anna exclaimed.

"I counted ten general stores, three hardware stores, and three lumberyards. Scotland's so big and thriving now, it's got two main streets.

"I tell you, everyone was talking nothing but land. People are just streaming into Dakota. They've even built a new flax mill that's going to make Scotland the center for flax in all the Dakota Territory and Minnesota, too. I saw the mill for myself. I've decided we'll grow flax for our cash crop, Becca."

Mr. Fency nodded his head in approval. "That's a good choice, they say. Especially on newly broken ground. And in late spring, when the flax blooms, the blue flowers make a real shimmering sight. Almost looks like one of the lakes back home in Michigan."

Anna nodded. "Tell us more about the town. How many churches are built now?"

"Why, I heard there were three. And Addie, they're talking about building a new school to replace the one the children use above one of the general stores."

Mother smiled. "A real school?"

"Is it going to be made of brick?" Addie asked.

"I don't know," Pa said, laughing. "One day I'm sure we'll have our own school right here in Hutchinson County that you and your brothers can walk to. I'll tell you, the area's really booming."

"But what about your house, Samuel?" Mr. Fency asked. "You know it takes nearly an acre of plowed sod to make enough bricks for a decent-sized soddy. Each brick weighs nearly fifty pounds. That's awful heavy work for just one man and woman and an eight-year-old boy."

"That's right," said Anna. "And it'll be snowing before you know it. That's why I think you should let us help you. If we work together you can have a neat fourteen-by-eighteen-foot house in no time at all."

"I'd say we could do it in a day and a half if we work without interruptions," Mr. Fency said.

"That's most generous of you," Pa said. "What do you think, Becca?"

"Well, I am worried about getting our house built. It would be most generous of the Fencys to help us, especially after all they've done already. Perhaps if Addie stayed here to look after the farm, the Fencys would feel better about leaving it for a day or two. We could take Lew and Nellie May, of course. But if Addie would watch Burt, he wouldn't be in our way and we'd be able to get the work done faster."

"Leaving Addie here to watch the Fencys' place and Burt makes a lot of sense," Pa agreed. "She's taken care of farm chores and the little ones all day while we worked in the fields back in Iowa. I think she could do it."

Addie kept her eyes down. Her heart was beating so loudly that she wondered if everyone else could hear it.

"The chickens and cows must be fed daily, and the cows must be milked. I'm afraid I couldn't go along if the livestock weren't being taken care of," Mr. Fency said.

"Then it's settled. Addie will stay behind with Burt. The rest of us will leave in the morning before sunrise," Pa said. "Once the house is close to finished, I'll ride for Addie and Burt. I should be back before night the day after tomorrow."

George smiled one of his most horrible smiles at Addie. He was going to the new claim and she wasn't. Addie tried not to look at her brother. She tried not to look at anyone because she felt two large tears beginning to roll down her face.

"Too bad you can't go with us and see the new land," George said, trying to appear sad and consoling but sounding very satisfied just the same. Then he added in a low, quiet voice only Addie could hear, "We just can't take along crybabies, I guess."

"I hate you, George," Addie whispered, wiping her face with her clenched fist. "I wish I would never see you again."

George smiled triumphantly and went outside to do his chores. Addie could hear him whistling even after he left the soddy.

It didn't matter that she felt frightened about staying alone on the Fency farm all day and overnight with just her little brother for company. Her family had to get their soddy built. It was almost November. In a few weeks the ground might be frozen solid. Addie felt herself shrinking, almost disappearing, as she sat on the nail keg. All she could think about was the Norwegian family, lost in a blizzard. What if it began snowing before Mother and Pa came back to get her?

What was left on her plate no longer seemed appetizing. Noticing that Addie had not finished her meal, Mother divided the remains between Lew and Burt, who quickly finished off the potatoes and pork. Pa and Mr. Fency went outside to the lean-to to check the cattle, and Lew and Burt bolted from the table to follow them. Still Addie sat silent.

"You'll be fine, Addie. You always manage very well with Burt. And you know how to take care of the livestock and keep the stove lit better than most girls twice your age," Mother said reassuringly as she picked up the empty plates. "I wish we didn't have to leave you here, but there's no other way to get our new house built."

Addie kept her eyes squarely on her lap. She reached for Ruby Lillian in her pocket.

"We'll only be gone a day and a half. Are you afraid?" her mother asked, lifting Addie's chin so that she could look directly in her eyes.

"No," Addie lied, ashamed of how frightened she really felt. "You're sure it will only be one night?"

"If it takes longer, I promise I'll come back by myself to get you. Somebody has to watch the farm while we're gone, and you know how hard it is to work with Burt underfoot. He's not like Lew. He doesn't understand where he isn't supposed to go. Taking care of the Fencys' farm is the least we can do for them after all the kindness they've shown us."

Addie nodded. She would try to be brave. But deep down inside Eleanor's taunt echoed, "Fraidycat, fraidy-cat . . .'"

# 9  FRAIDYCAT

In the early morning darkness, Addie watched the two wagons until they disappeared on the northwestern horizon. Her family had taken all their supplies, Big Jones, and the oxen, which would be needed to pull the breaking plow through the tough sod. From the soddy roof, Addie waved her sunbonnet over and over again, straining her eyes to see a glimmer of white, some other sunbonnet—maybe Anna's or her mother's. Maybe if she tried hard enough, she could make out Mr. Fency's tall shape. In a few minutes they would all be out of sight. Addie sighed. Already she missed them—everyone, of course, except George. She didn't care if she never saw him again.

When every trace of her family and the Fencys was gone, Addie remained on the roof for a long time, watching the place where they had disappeared. She reminded herself of what Pa had said about being resourceful. She knew she could take care of Burt and the cows and chickens. And she certainly no longer feared Indians the way she once had. But it was the thought of spending the night alone that troubled her. The prairie was so black, even when there were stars and a moon. There were no neighbors' lights nearby, the way there had been in Sabula. She would be alone with Burt in a house without a door, listening to the terrible howling of the wolves.

"Eleanor was right. I *am* a fraidycat," Addie said to Ruby Lillian. Her smile did not seem reassuring today.

Addie climbed down off the roof and went inside to nibble on a cold biscuit and butter. She checked her brother, who was still sleeping, then she filled a bowl with some of the oatmeal Anna had left on the back of the stove. She propped her doll on the table against a tin cup as she ate breakfast. "Now Ruby Lillian, remember what I told you." Addie imitated the voice of Mr. Fency. "Milk the cows, give them fresh hay and water, strain the milk, and carry the milk pans to the root cellar to let the cream rise. Feed the chickens and gather the eggs. Watch Burt so he doesn't wander too close to the well or tip over a lighted dish of tallow. Don't let the fire go out, and be sure you skim the cream from the milk when it's cool. Can you remember all that, Ruby Lillian?"

When she had finished her breakfast, Addie sat at the table, drumming her fingers. Even with all the chores, it was still going to be a long day. Mother had left her a sampler to practice her stitches on. And there were always more cats to twist, but right now Addie did not feel like doing much of anything—not even cleaning up her breakfast dishes.

"And don't forget to sweep up the old grass from the soddy and lay down some new dried grass on the floor," she reminded Ruby Lillian, picking up the broom made of stiff hay bound to the end of a stick. With a sigh, Addie began sweeping. Building a new house seemed much more exciting than staying behind and taking care of Burt. If there were someone here like Eleanor to talk to, at least then the time might pass more quickly.

As she swept, Addie had an idea. She turned the broom upside down and put her bonnet on the stiff bristles. She tied the bonnet, wrapped an apron around the broom handle, and leaned the broom against the table.

"So nice of you to join us this morning," she said to her new companion. "Miss Primrose, please meet Miss Ruby Lillian."

The broom in the sunbonnet was very polite but rather shy. Nonetheless, Addie was pleased that Miss Primrose and Ruby Lillian seemed to get along so well, especially since this was the first time they'd met. "Would you care for tea or coffee?" Addie said, placing two tin cups on the table. "I'm sorry I can only offer you sugar. We have no lemons this time of year," she apologized, using the same words she remembered her mother saying when the minister came to call last spring. Addie imagined Miss Primrose nodding politely and sipping her tea. "You know the price of store-bought sugar is very dear these days," she added. She waited for Miss Primrose to answer.

When she couldn't think of anything for Miss Primrose to say, Addie sat down at the table with her chin in her hands. She wished her brother would wake up so that there'd be someone real to talk to. She was beginning to feel a little nervous all by herself. She touched the Indian necklace around her neck. Maybe she wasn't brave enough to wear a special eagle feather. She hesitated for a moment but decided to keep the necklace on after all. Maybe she would feel braver if she were busy. "After all, it *is* time to milk the cows," she reminded herself and went to the lean-to with a metal bucket.

Bess and Missy seemed to look at her in surprise as she sat down on the Fencys' milking stool. The smell of sweet grass and warm cows filled the little shed, making Addie feel safe and comfortable. She had been milking cows since she was six, and it was a chore she knew how to do very well. Little by little the metal bucket filled, ringing with a tinny sound as the spray of milk hit its sides.

When she was done, Addie carried the milk to the soddy and strained it carefully with a sieve into pans. She lifted the trap door in one corner of the soddy's floor. This led to the root cellar, a hole that extended under the lean-to.

She placed a dish of tallow with a rag lit in it near the edge of the trap-door opening, just as she had seen Anna do. Then she stepped down the short ladder into the cellar, carrying one pan of milk at a time. The root cellar was four feet deep, large enough for the Fencys to store two or three barrels and several bushel baskets and wooden boxes of food. In the boxes were carrots covered with sand, crocks of cooked pork sealed with lard, dried corn, and jars of canned cabbage, plums, green beans, tomatoes, and watermelon pickles. Cabbage heads hung from the ceiling by their roots. The root cellar was dark and cool, and Addie did not like to stay down there long because of the way the tallow light threw shadows on the walls. She set the pans of milk on top of a barrel and hurried back up the ladder. Quickly she replaced the trap door and went outside to give the cows fresh hay and water.

When Burt woke up, Addie gave him a bowl of oatmeal with plenty of corn sweetener. "Mama?" he asked, pounding the table with his sticky spoon.

"Mama will be back soon," Addie said, dabbing a corner of her apron with water and wiping oatmeal from her brother's hair. "You look a mess, Burt." She pulled his damp flannel shirt-dress over his head and put a clean one on him. She didn't want Burt to get sick with the croup from wearing wet clothes.

Her brother watched her while she rinsed the little shirt and rubbed it with soap against the washboard. He followed her outside as she carried the basket of damp laundry Anna had washed the night before. When she was finished hanging everything on the line, Burt helped his sister search for eggs in the tall grass around the soddy. While they were looking, Addie found a spiderweb delicately stretched between some butterfly milkweeds and the dried stalk of a sunflower. Droplets of dew clung to the web and shimmered in the morning light. She and Eleanor had called these "fairy necklaces" whenever they found them in the forest near the Mills's farm in Jackson County. "Pretty, isn't it?" Addie asked Burt. Her brother didn't seem interested. He was waving a stick at a chicken. Addie wished Eleanor were here to share the sight of the fairy necklace with her.

Addie went back inside and greased the two eggs she had found with lard the way Anna had shown her. She buried them in the barrel filled with grain in the root cellar. "The cows have been fed, the floor swept," she said looking to Miss Primrose for approval. "How am I doing?"

Addie spent the rest of the morning outside, building a little castle of stones and sticks for Ruby Lillian and Burt. She had seen a castle in one of Eleanor's books. The parts of the castle she couldn't remember, she just made up. Little by little the building grew in a patch of bare, dry ground outside the soddy.

It was a bright, warm Indian summer day. Because the weather was so pleasant, they ate a picnic lunch of biscuits and cheese near the new castle. "Careful, Burt, don't knock it down just yet," she told her brother as she carefully placed a flag of dry Indian grass between two stones. "Oh, Burt! Now see what you've done!" Addie cried, rescuing Ruby Lillian from underneath a fallen castle wall.

Burt sheepishly removed his foot from the center of the castle. His bottom lip trembled as he stared at the ruins. He looked as if he might begin crying at any moment. Before he had a chance, Addie let out a wild whoop and gathered him in her arms. With Burt slung over her shoulder, she galloped out past the firebreak until he laughed and laughed.

In the evening Addie finished the last of the day's chores. She skimmed the cream from the milk in the root cellar and made a dinner of pearled barley cooked in buttermilk. "Tomorrow we'll go looking for prairie dog houses," she told her brother as she smoothed his hair and pulled his quilt over his shoulders. At least she had Burt for company, she thought.

Addie lit a piece of rag in a dish of tallow and set this on the table. Then she made sure the canvas flaps at the door and window were pulled tight to keep the prairie night out. She took out her sampler and began practicing the stitches her mother had taught her. Addie worked one row of cross-stitch that was a border for the alphabet.

"How do you like my cross-stitch, Ruby Lillian? Or do you think my running stitch is better?" Addie asked. Ruby Lillian smiled from her perch atop the wooden cracker box but remained silent. Addie sighed. What fun were friends if they couldn't say anything?

It was hard to make the stitches even in the dim light. She put the sampler away and opened Anna's trunk. Anna had told her she could read the books if she were careful Burt didn't touch them. She admired the beautiful color pictures in *Aesop's Fables*. It seemed a luxury to read without being interrupted by anyone. But somehow tonight not even the tortoise and the hare could make her forget that she and Burt were all alone.

Burt snored loudly and uncurled from a tight ball. Addie listened hard. Beyond the walls of the soddy, beyond the flimsy canvas covering the doorway and the window, she could hear it beginning, the sound she had been dreading. The wolves were howling. She covered her ears with her hands, but the mournful sound would not go away.

Addie placed a few more twisted cats into the fire. She left the rag light burning on the table and pushed Anna's trunk and a nail keg against the doorway. Then she kicked off her shoes and tucked Ruby Lillian under her pillow. She took up Anna's heavy rolling pin and crawled in under the covers next to Burt. She didn't even bother to change into her nightclothes. If the wolves came, she would be ready to defend herself and her brother with the only weapon left in the house—the rolling pin. More than ever she wished that Pa had taught her how to shoot. If only he hadn't taken the gun!

Addie pulled the quilt up over her ears and waited for sleep to come, clutching the rolling pin in one hand. Instead of sleeping, she could only stare at the shadows on the flap over the doorway. She shut her eyes and listened to her brother snore. Nothing seemed to be frightening him. Addie began counting his snores and little by little felt herself growing drowsy.

The next thing she knew she was waking up, and there was light coming in around the edges of the canvas at the window. She had survived the night alone. She sat up and stretched. The rolling pin had fallen out of her hand in the night and rolled under the bed. She had not needed it after all. The wolves' howling was gone and so was the prairie's darkness.

Quietly, so as not to wake Burt, she climbed out of bed and splashed her face with a handful of water from the bucket. She threw more cats into the stove and filled a kettle with water to make tea. Then she went outside. The morning air felt cold and she could see her breath in little white puffs. But there was no frost, only dew clinging to the dried grass.

When Addie had finished the milking and her other morning chores, she prepared a breakfast of gruel for herself and Burt. Carefully she dropped pinches of cornmeal into the boiling water. She felt pleased about how well she was doing on her own.

"Don't you think I'm doing just fine?" she asked Ruby Lillian, as she took her out from beneath the pillow and placed her on the table. Addie spooned gruel into two bowls.

"Mama! Mama!" Burt demanded.

"She'll be back, Burt. Pa's coming to get us soon as he can." Addie sighed. It still seemed like a long, long time to wait for her parents to return. But she had made it through the night. The worst was over.

She washed the breakfast dishes, swept, read Burt a story from Anna's book, and then took him outside to look for prairie dogs.

In the afternoon while Burt napped, Addie worked on her sampler again. Suddenly she heard low bellows from the cows. What was the matter with Bess and Missy? A gust of wind blew into the soddy, knocking the canvas flap against the wall. Addie looked outside. The sky seemed unusually dark for this time of the afternoon. Or had she lost track of time? Was it later than she thought?

The wind blew dust through the yard, and the cows continued making frightened noises. Addie hurried to the clothesline to make sure the laundry she had forgotten on the line since yesterday had not blown away. She gathered the bedding and Burt's clothes. Pulling the flapping sheets away from her face, she saw a queer sight in the south-western sky. The far horizon was ablaze with orange and yellow, as if the sun were setting.

But Addie knew exactly where the sun set. She had watched the western horizon every day since they left Iowa. This glow wasn't from the sun.

She bundled the laundry together and tossed it inside the soddy, then scrambled up the ladder to the roof for a better look. As she climbed, the wind grew stronger. She crawled along the roof, shielding her eyes from flying dust and sharp pieces of brittle grass. A family of coyotes raced through Mr. Fency's plowed field, not even stopping to bother Anna's chickens, who frantically clucked near the lean-to. Addie wiped her eyes with her apron and discovered that her face was covered with black flecks. There were cinders flying in the air! The bright glow she saw was a prairie fire, and it was headed right for the Fency farm.

The palms of her hands broke into a cold sweat. She had to think of a way to save herself and Burt. She had to think of a way to save the farm. She scrambled off the roof and ran inside the soddy to wake her brother.

"Burt! Wake up!" she screamed. "We've got to get out of here!"

Burt's eyes flew open, and he began to whimper. He knew something was terribly wrong as he watched his sister gather Anna's books and stuff them back into the trunk. With all her strength she pushed the trunk across the room and opened the trap door to the root cellar. She shoved the trunk into the cellar with one terrific push. There was barely enough room for it. Neither she nor Burt would fit down there as well. She slammed the door.

"Where are we going to hide? What are we going to do?" she blurted and ran outside. The wind swept across the yard, picking up dried leaves and pieces of grass and sending them into the sky in little corkscrew formations. Addie remembered what Pa had said about a stiff wind behind a prairie fire. Would the Fencys' firebreak save them? The cows were bellowing in terror now. Addie decided to untie Bess and Missy and let them run from the fire. Their eyes rolled as they pulled against their ropes. "Run as fast as you can!" Addie shouted, hitting each cow on the rump. Should she and Burt try to run, too? But how far could they get in bare feet?

Addie raced back into the soddy and put on her black, copper-toed boots. She quickly slipped Burt's shoes on him. Pulling him by the hand, she ran outside again. They were past the firebreak, running away from the fire as fast as Addie could go, when she realized she had left Ruby Lillian behind on the table. She picked Burt up and dashed back. The soddy's darkness and quiet made the fire seem farther away. She wanted to stay there, but she knew she couldn't. From the door she could see that the approaching flames were as tall as three houses stacked one atop the other. The wind was so strong the firebreak would never work. She knew there wasn't time to set a backfire, even if she knew how.

"A fire can't go where there's nothing to burn." Addie repeated Pa's words frantically, trying to think of a plan. She crouched and motioned to her brother. "Get on my back, Burt." The child sobbed tearfully but did as he was told.

She ran outside with Burt on her back and Ruby Lillian in her pocket. The wall of fire was closer; she could see tufts of grass exploding into flames. With each explosion the sky filled with more and more billows of black smoke. The roar was deafening, like a terrible, rolling summer thunderstorm.

"I promised to watch the farm and keep it safe," she told Burt, placing him on the ground near the well. "I can't let the Fencys' house burn." She lowered bucket after bucket into the water, soaking the soddy's walls as best she could. But even as she desperately tossed water, more pieces of burning grass landed on the roof. Saving the soddy seemed hopeless. Addie pulled the ladder away from the house and threw it on the ground just as it was about to catch fire, too. She would never be able to keep the house from burning all by herself.

Addie was exhausted, but she kept hauling bucket after bucket up the well as best she could. She could not think. Her arms kept working as if she had no control over them. As she pulled up one more bucket, she saw her reflection in the water, illuminated by the fire's glow. She and Burt had only a few minutes before the sea of flames would engulf them. Where could she find a place

to hide from those awful, devouring explosions? "Where's there nothing to burn," Addie whispered. Suddenly she knew what to do. She dragged the ladder to the well, the way she had done to save her doll, Eleanor. She pushed it down inside.

Burt was crying hysterically, crouched on the ground with his hands over his ears to stop the horrible noise. "Come on, Burt, we have to hurry. Climb on my back," Addie shouted.

"No, NO!" Burt sobbed.

"You have to!" Addie commanded. She knelt beside her brother. Reluctantly he grabbed around her shoulders, crying harder than ever.

Still kneeling on the ground, Addie used one foot to carefully feel for the ladder's highest rung. Slowly, she lowered herself, balancing Burt with great effort. Down into the well she went, step over step. Now they were below ground level. It was pitch black, and the water felt cold around Addie's knees as she reached the bottom rung. "Don't let go, Burt. Don't let go," she told her brother, who buried his face into the back of her neck so that her necklace dug deep into her skin.

The terrible roar of the fire grew louder. Addie wanted to cover both her ears, but she could not let go. She had to hold on tight to the ladder while standing as still as possible. Any minute the fire would be right over them. What would happen then. Would they melt? She remained motionless even as several stones and a handful of dirt came loose from the wall and tumbled into the water. Was the well going to cave in on them?

Now the noise was deafening. Pieces of burning grass hissed as they fell into the well water, just missing the children. Cinders smarted Addie's eyes. How long? How long until the fire came? Addie glanced up just as the flames roared over the mouth of the well.

# 10 TRAPPED!

Addie held her breath and closed her eyes. For one brief, horrible moment she was certain her hair would catch fire. The hot white light charged overhead with a howling ten times worse than the loudest locomotive Addie had ever heard. But as quickly as the flames appeared, they were gone.

A gust of wind blew more cinders and smoke into the well, and the children began coughing. Around the edge of the well, where Mr. Fency had laid sod bricks, Addie could see a few small flames sputter and go out as the last piece of dry grass was consumed.

"Burt? Are you all right?" she asked in a hoarse whisper.

"Mama! Mama!" his voice echoed in the well. He clung to Addie even more tightly.

Her legs shook in the cold water. A terrible pain shot up and down her back where her brother dug in with his knees. But still she did not move or change position. She felt as if she were frozen, clinging to the ladder for dear life. Nearly half an hour passed. There was no more roar to be heard, even in the distance, and the air seemed filled with an almost eerie silence.

Addie whispered again, "Burt, are you all right? I'm going to climb back up now. Don't touch the walls. Don't touch anything. Just hold on tight to me."

Addie climbed up one step. Then another. She stopped as some rocks tumbled past and splashed in the water. Burt whimpered and coughed. The top of the well seemed almost farther than Addie could manage. She was exhausted. Burt felt heavier by the minute, even though he weighed only a bit more than twenty-five pounds. If only Pa would come now and lift them both out. If only he would save them.

"Addie!" Burt cried, his voice echoing. "Out! Out!"

"Hush, Burt!" Addie hissed as a small section of the well wall crumbled and collapsed above them, sending dirt all over their faces and hair.

Pa wasn't going to save them. The only way they could get out was if she climbed out herself, with Burt on her back. Somehow she'd just have to trust that she could make it all nine feet up to the top. "Hold on, Burt. We're almost there," she said, her voice cracking. Only four more steps.

Suddenly Addie heard a familiar voice.

"Addie! Addie! Where are you?" someone called desperately.

It wasn't Pa. It was George!

"We're in the well!" Addie shouted. Another pile of dirt splashed into the water.

A face peered down at her. "Grab hold of my hand," George said, throwing his coat over the charred sod at the well's edge and lying on his stomach, his arms reaching down to them. "Careful now. Not too fast."

The ladder teetered as she reached the top-most rung. Addie made a desperate lunge for George's hands and solid ground. As her foot left the top rung, one side of the wall began to crumble. A section of stones and dirt broke loose and crashed into the water. Addie threw herself forward, grasped the well's edge with both hands, and scrambled to safe ground. Burt tumbled from her back, unharmed.

Addie hugged George as Burt jumped up and down with excitement. She couldn't believe how happy she was to see him. Her brother seemed just as happy to see her.

"You should take a look at yourself, Addie," George said, grinning. "Your face is black as a skunk's. Yours, too, Burt. Mother will hardly recognize you."

"Pa and Mother are all right? What about the others? You didn't get caught in the fire?" Addie asked anxiously.

"The fire passed to the south of us, heading straight east on the other side of the river. We were on our way back when we saw it coming. We headed to get you two as fast as we could travel. I rode ahead of the others to look for you. You sure scared me, Addie. When I got to the soddy, all I found was a burned scrap of your sunbonnet." George held out what was left of the bonnet Addie had used to decorate Miss Primrose. "I thought I'd never see you again."

"You won't get rid of me that easily, George Sidney," Addie said. She looked sheepishly at the toes of her dirty, wet boots. "I'm sorry about what I said to you before you left. I don't really hate you."

George blushed. "You aren't a crybaby, either. I just said that to be mean. You're about the bravest person I know. I don't believe I'd have been able to figure what to do if I'd gotten caught in a prairie fire."

"You really think I'm brave?" Addie asked, suddenly feeling wonderful in spite of her damp clothes and aching back. "But you know, George, I *was* afraid down there." She hesitated. "And I was afraid when the Indians came here, too."

"Maybe you were scared, but you did something courageous anyway. I think that's what being brave's all about."

Addie was quiet for a moment. "Maybe the Indian necklace helped. Pa said it was special. I'll let you wear it sometime, if you want."

George looked pleased. "I'd like that, Addie. I'd like that a lot."

The children stepped over the smoldering black stubs that had once been Anna's garden. The fire had raced far enough to the east so that it was now a steady glow in the distance. The Fency soddy was charred black, but it was still standing. The prairie all around continued smoking. The ground was covered with blackened patches of brittle, burned grass, and the air was filled with the bitter, acrid smell of smoke. As they walked, the scorched ground crackled under their feet.

Addie looked in every direction and saw how horrible the firestorm had been. Straightening her shoulders, she felt a sudden pride. If she hadn't acted as quickly as she had, they would have been killed. Climbing into the well had been her own magnificent, new, wonderful idea. She had been very brave, just as George had said. She had saved her brother and herself. That was something, wasn't it? She had survived an Indian visit all alone, too. Dakota didn't seem quite so frightening anymore. Maybe Eleanor was wrong. Maybe she *was* a sodbusting pioneer-type after all.

The wagon and horses rumbled into what was left of the Fencys' yard, and Pa and Mother leapt quickly to the ground.

"Lord be praised! Lord be praised!" Mother kept saying, hugging the children and kissing their faces over and over as if she couldn't believe they were really there. "Are you all right? How did you manage to get through that fire alive? It came up so fast! If I'd thought anything so terrible could have happened, I never would have left you here alone. Never!" She burst into tears, and that was the second time Addie had ever seen her mother cry.

"Found them in the well, Mother," George said, awkwardly patting his mother's shoulder. "They were standing on the ladder."

"So you climbed into the well, Addie. That was a wise thing to do, a very wise thing. If you'd gone anywhere else, I just...I just don't know," Pa said in a broken voice, gathering Addie up in his arms even though she was much too big to be carried. "You saved your brother's life as well as your own. The firebreak couldn't hold off those flames. The wind was too strong."

Anna had gone inside the soddy, and Mr. Fency was poking about the yard and the lean-to, trying to see what was left. He came over to Addie and her family, his shoulders stooped. He did not look as tall as he once had. "Fire was so hot, it melted my plow handles. My seed for next year's planting is gone. I found the carcasses of Bess and Missy. The house is still standing, but everything inside was destroyed."

"I let the cows go. It was my fault," said Addie sadly. "I thought they'd have a better chance running away from the fire."

"You did the best thing, little sister," Mr. Fency said slowly. "The firebreak couldn't have held up against a fire moving that fast. And there's no way you could have gotten the cows down inside the well. I'm only glad you and Burt are safe."

"Addie's a plucky little gal," Pa said. "Mr. Fency, you and Anna can come back with us. We'll finish our soddy while things cool off here. Then George and I will help you get settled again. In the spring you can use my plow and some of my seed. I've got more than enough."

From the house there came a moan, and Anna appeared, her eyes red from crying. "Everything inside's destroyed, even my trunk. All my fine things burned. Everything I brought from Michigan—all our photographs, our winter clothing, our bedding and linens. Things I've had since we were first married. Everything's gone." She wiped her eyes with her apron. Mother put her arm around Anna.

Addie slipped away, feeling as though it were all her fault that she hadn't been able to save any of the Fencys' things. What had happened to the trunk? She entered the smoke-filled soddy and kicked away the burned grass and the remains of the Fencys' table and bed. She found the trap door to the root cellar. It was so charred that when she kicked hard, it fell apart.

"Anna! Mr. Fency!" Addie called as she stuck her head down into the root cellar.

With help from Pa, Mr. Fency lifted the big trunk out of the root cellar and carried it into the yard. Anna opened it and stared in disbelief. Everything inside was safe.

"And the provisions we stored in the cellar aren't touched either," Mr. Fency said, his face beaming.

"You still have Ruby Lillian, too," Addie said. She reached in her pocket and carefully placed Ruby Lillian in Anna's hand.

Again, Anna's eyes filled with tears as she turned the doll over and over in her hands. "Thanks to you, Addie, I have much, much more. I have you and Burt." She put her arms around Addie. "If we'd all been here when that fire came, we never would have all fit in that well, that's for certain. Who knows if any of us would have survived? You keep Ruby Lillian for me, will you? You saved her life, too."

# 11  HOME TO OAK HOLLOW

Addie watched her father and Mr. Fency load what was left of the Fencys' provisions into the wagon.

"Climb in!" Pa called. The children squeezed into the wagon with Anna, Mother, and Nellie May. The baby's eyes were wide and curious as she peered over Mother's shoulder at Addie. Addie smiled at Nellie May and touched her soft pink cheek with her finger.

"We going?" Burt asked, snuggling close to Addie.

"We're going home to Oak Hollow," Addie replied, watching the Fency farm disappear behind a blackened rise of prairie that stretched nearly to one horizon. When they reached the river, Addie could see the swells of ground that the flames had left untouched. The wagon crossed the river, and the horses struggled to pull the wagon up the bank.

Ahead, a flock of Canada geese leaped from the ground and soared higher and higher into the sky, moving together almost as if one bird. Addie felt as free as the geese, capable of doing anything she set her mind to. Living here was hard, but she felt as if now she could meet the prairie's challenge.

For the first time since they'd left Jackson County, Iowa, Addie could hardly wait to see what their family's new one hundred sixty acres looked like. Would there be any trees to play in? Would there be a stream nearby to float pirate ships? Was it true what Anna had said, that the prairie would bloom in the spring more beautiful than any garden back in Sabula?

"Beulah Land, sweet Beulah Land," Mother began singing, as she drew Burt and Addie close beside her. "Upon the highest rock I stand."

At the chorus Anna joined in, and the women's clear voices rose up and seemed to hover above the wagon like the smoke that had lingered after the fire.

> *I look away across the sea*
> *where mansions are prepared for me*
> *and view the shining glory there,*
> *my heavenly home forevermore.*

"Home," Addie whispered to Ruby Lillian. "We're going home." Holding her necklace feather in her hand, Addie closed her eyes and made a wish. She wished that one of their new neighbors would be a girl her own age. Somehow, she just knew her wish would come true.